SANDPIPER

SANDPIPER

Ellen Wittlinger

5/04 TBiT 16.95

SIMON & SCHUSTER BOOKS FOR YOUNG READERS

New York   London   Toronto   Sydney

Also by Ellen Wittlinger:

Heart on My Sleeve

Zigzag

The Long Night of Leo and Bree

Razzle

What's in a Name

Hard Love

Gracie's Girl

SIMON & SCHUSTER BOOKS FOR YOUNG READERS
An imprint of Simon & Schuster Children's Publishing Division
1230 Avenue of the Americas, New York, New York 10020

SIMON & SCHUSTER BOOKS FOR YOUNG READERS is a trademark of Simon & Schuster, Inc.
Book design by Greg Stadnyk
The text for this book is set in Janson Text.
Manufactured in the United States of America
10 9 8 7 6 5 4 3 2 1
Library of Congress Cataloging-in-Publication Data
Wittlinger, Ellen.
Sandpiper / Ellen Wittlinger.— 1st ed.
p. cm.
Summary: When the Walker, a mysterious boy who walks constantly, intervenes in an argument between Sandpiper and a boy she used to see, their lives become entwined in ways that change them both.
ISBN 0-689-86802-2 (hardcover)
[1. Dating (Social custom)—Fiction 2. Interpersonal relations—Fiction. 3. Walking—Fiction.]
I. Title.
PZ7.W78436Wal 2005
[Fic]—dc22
2004007576

FIRST
F
EDITION

For Diane Wald
who reminded me where poetry can take you

With grateful thanks to my editor, David Gale; his assistant, Alexandra Cooper; my agent, Ginger Knowlton, and Pat Lowery Collins, Anita Riggio, and Nancy Werlin for their help and advice on the manuscript.

Special thanks to the Fine Arts Work Center in Provincetown, Massachusetts.

Chapter ONE

I met the Walker three weeks before my mother's wedding, but I'd seen him lots of times before that. Everybody saw him. You couldn't help it.

It seemed like he just showed up one day and started walking all over town. No certain path—you'd see him everywhere, way in the west end near the Y, all the way south on Beggar's Point by Pickford's Fish, or sometimes stalking through the cemetery on the top of Rhodes Hill. He didn't walk fast or slow, just at a regular pace, like he had someplace to go but wasn't in a big hurry to get there. Nobody knew his name, so we started calling him the Walker.

You noticed him because he was tall and skinny, and even though he didn't walk fast, he covered ground quickly with his long stride. His dark hair curled around his earlobes and down his neck, and he always wore the same ancient brown leather jacket, his long arms sticking about four inches out of the sleeves. The day I met him it was almost warm out, and he had his coat unzipped. I was with this guy Andrew down at Blessingame Park, and we were arguing.

To tell the story right, I need to back up a little. The thing is, even though he was a very annoying person, I'd hooked up with Andrew for a couple of days. We'd go to his house after school because his parents worked late. Colleen, my mother, was way too discombobulated about her upcoming wedding to inquire about my after-school activities.

I don't know why I went with Andrew. I was never particularly attracted to him, but every time I saw him he'd tell me he thought I was hot. He'd come up behind me and rub his thigh against mine while I was getting stuff out of my locker.

I'm not stupid. I knew why he wanted me to go home with him, and I was up for it right away. I usually *am* up for it. The thing is, I love the beginning stuff when the guy is so anxious and can hardly wait to be alone with me, can hardly wait to have me touch him. All that expectation is very exciting. And it makes me feel like I'm in control of the whole situation. He needs me *so much*.

But it always ends up the same way. Eventually it's clear that what he *really* needs is for me to put my mouth around his dick. After a minute or two of this I become anonymous. To the guy and to myself. Andrew (or whoever) is lost inside himself, waiting to be shaken by his own little volcano, and I'm thinking, *Who is this girl kneeling on the floor with some weird guy's bone in her mouth?* It's like I'm not even there anymore.

It all started in the eighth grade. That year all of a sudden you had to have a boyfriend—you *had* to, or you just felt worthless. My best friends, Melissa and Allie, and I spent hours talking about how to get guys to like us.

Melissa was the first one to figure out a foolproof method. Allie and I were disgusted when she confessed to us why Tim

McIlhenny was following her around like an imprinted duck. But after a few weeks of listening to Melissa's detailed instructions, we both decided to give it a try. Who knew? Obviously, the way to an eighth-grade boy's heart was through the zipper of his jeans. It probably wasn't the only way, but it was the only way we knew.

Tony Phillips was my slave for two months. He even took me to the Christmas dance that year. Some days I felt like a princess and some days I felt like a prostitute, but every day I felt popular. I went from Tony to Chris to Evan. And kept on going. Melissa assured Allie and me that *lots* of other girls were doing the same thing we were (although I never knew who), which is what I planned to tell my parents if they ever found out. But they never did.

In high school things changed—at least for Melissa and Allie. They took honors classes, joined the student council and the field hockey team, and got real boyfriends who stuck around for a while. We didn't hang out so much anymore. For me there was always another guy, and then another. I don't know why things changed for them but not for me. What I do know is that after a week or so with a guy, even somebody I was crazy about to begin with, I couldn't stand him anymore. With Andrew it took only three days.

That's what we were arguing about in Blessingame Park.

"You liked me well enough on Tuesday," he said.

"Yeah, well, today is Thursday," I told him. "A lot can happen in two days."

"Like what? You're with somebody else now?"

"Jesus, Andrew, I was never *with you!* Did you think we were engaged?"

"Screw you, Sandy."

I gave him a forlorn look. "Oh, I bet you wish you could!"

His face turned bright red, and his nose twisted up so I could see into his nostrils. "You are such a slut!" he shrieked, his voice breaking into a falsetto over the horror that was me.

Just about that time I noticed the Walker coming up the hill in back of Andrew. He must have heard Andrew shrieking at me, because he was staring right at us. Without really thinking about it too much, I waved at him and yelled out, "Hey! I've been waiting for you!"

He looked surprised, but he didn't say anything. His hair was flopping into his face as if he hadn't had a haircut in ages.

"Come here!" I yelled again. I thought, if he came over, great; if not, I was no worse off.

Andrew turned to see who I was talking to. "What are you calling him over for?"

"*Because!*" God, Andrew not only couldn't take a hint—he couldn't take a brickbat to the head.

The Walker strode over and stood next to me, his eyes asking what this was all about. Andrew backed up to stare—the Walker was quite a bit taller. "I know you. You're that guy who just wanders around town all the time."

"Yeah, I walk around a lot. Who are you?"

Andrew sputtered. "Well, why should I tell you?"

"You shouldn't. You should probably just leave."

Ha! He *got* it! He was following my lead!

"*I* should leave?" Andrew stood there with his mouth flapping in the breeze. Repartee is not his strong suit. "I mean, you're the one who should leave. Right?" He looked at me.

I was *so* sick of this guy. How could I have spent three

entire afternoons with him? I stepped closer to the Walker and put my hand on his wrist. "Actually, no, he shouldn't," I said. I could feel the muscles tighten in his arm, but he didn't move.

Once again, Andrew couldn't get his mind around a complete thought. "What? You don't mean . . . do you mean . . . no way!"

The Walker placed his hand over my hand, but he didn't say anything.

Finally, Andrew had had enough. "I don't know why I ever went out with you anyway, Sandy. Derek told me you were a bitch, and he was right!"

"Bite me, Andrew!" I yelled back. "Derek is as pathetic as you are." *Derek*. Last week's loser. Another guy I never should have gotten involved with.

Andrew stalked out of the park and down Front Street.

As soon as Andrew was out of sight, the Walker let go of my hand and I released his arm.

"Thanks," I said. "Sorry about that."

He shrugged again. "No problem." And he started to walk away.

"Hold on. Can we talk a minute? Or something?" Two minutes ago I'd decided to swear off boys—I didn't need the aggravation—and then the Walker showed up. It's so easy for me to get interested in a boy; all he has to do is look at me. Not that the Walker had actually looked at me, but he *was* sort of my superhero savior. Or he would have been if Andrew had been evil instead of just a creep.

"I like to keep moving," he said.

"Well, can I walk with you a little while?"

He didn't say anything, but then he gave another shrug—apparently this was his primary means of communication, the I-don't-care shrug. It wasn't exactly a warm invitation, but I took it anyway, and we started walking out of the park in the opposite direction from the one that Andrew had taken.

"I've seen you walking around town," I said.

"I guess everybody has."

"How come you walk so much?"

Another shrug. "I like walking. I notice things."

He didn't seem to be noticing *me* all that much. "What's your name?"

He shook his head. "It's not important."

I laughed. "It must be some regular, common name then, because if it was as stupid as my name, it would be *very* important, believe me."

He looked at me for the first time—at least I'd accomplished *that*. "Why? What's your name?"

Normally I dread this moment when meeting somebody new, but this time I was glad I had something to say that would get his attention, maybe even stop the Walker in his tracks.

"Sandpiper Hollow Ragsdale."

A hint of a smile crossed his face, but he kept on walking. "Did you just make that up?"

"I wish! That's my honest-to-God name. Hollow in the middle, like a cheap chocolate Easter bunny." I've used that line many times—it usually gets a laugh.

He smiled again, but not in my direction. "Your parents must have had a good reason for naming you that. Or an odd sense of humor."

"Both. They met on this beach on Cape Cod called Sandpiper Hollow. Colleen stepped on a broken shell and cut her foot. Love walked in and kissed her boo-boo, and they named their firstborn child after the unforgettable moment."

The Walker nodded. "Makes a good story."

"Yeah, with a terrible ending! Just because two people manage to make a baby, I don't think they should have the right to give it a name that's just an inside joke between the two of them, which, once they get divorced, won't be all that funny anymore."

"Parents divorced?"

"Years ago. A sandpiper is a bird, you know."

"I know."

"I guess I'm lucky they didn't name me Nuthatch or Buzzard or something."

"Or Woodpecker," the Walker said. Hey, he could make a joke.

"Or Cuckoo," I continued.

"Or Cedar Waxwing."

"Cedar what?"

"Cedar Waxwing."

"That's a bird? I never heard of that one. I kind of like it though. *Hello, my name is Cedar Waxwing.* I like it!"

The Walker pointed toward an old broken wire fence behind a new ranch house. "Did you know there's an old rail bed back there? You can follow it from Hammond all the way up to Barlow."

"No, I didn't know that." I hated being interrupted when I was on a roll about the injustice of my name.

"I walk it at least once a week."

"The whole thing? It must be five or six miles."

"Seven and a half each way," he said.

"Why?"

Of course, he answered with a shrug. "Why not?"

I sighed. He liked being a puzzle. And he certainly didn't seem interested in me. Maybe he wasn't worth the effort. "Don't you drive anywhere? How old are you?"

His head jerked up as if he'd seen something in the road, but there was no traffic on this street in the middle of the afternoon. Finally he said, "I'm eighteen, but I don't drive. I don't even ride in cars."

"What? You're crazy!"

He glanced at me and smiled. I liked that smile. "Probably," he said. "I hate cars."

"How can you hate *cars*! In four weeks I can get my license. I'm counting the days! I'll be *free*!"

"Walking gives you freedom."

I shook my head. "It's not the same."

He was quiet for a moment. Then he said, "So, people call you Sandy."

"How do you know that?"

"That's the name your . . . your friend used."

"First of all, that jerk is *not* my friend. And second, I hate the name Sandy. It's the name of Little Orphan Annie's *dog*. The kids at school use it, but I make my parents call me Sandpiper since they're the ones who stuck me with the name to begin with."

I swear a little grunt of laughter escaped from the guy. "So, that wasn't your boyfriend, huh?"

My face crinkled in disgust. "*Boy*friend? God, no. He's just somebody I hooked up with for a few days. I hardly even know him. He's nobody."

But the Walker had stopped listening to me; he'd actually stopped walking. He bent down to the street to examine some black lines. "Somebody put on their brakes really hard here. Took the corner too fast. These skid marks weren't here yesterday." He shook his head. "This is a blind corner too. I hope nobody got hurt."

I looked around. "I don't think I've ever been on this street."

"We're just down from Davis Avenue. You know, you better go on back. I'll lead you right out of town if you're not careful." He stood up and stared at me with eyes that were suddenly dull, like the lights had gone off behind them.

"I don't care! I like walking—"

He shook his head and looked back down at the tire marks. "Not today."

"Really! I can—"

"No! Go back now," he ordered. He seemed to be shivering. Even though it wasn't cold, he zipped up his coat. "Maybe I'll see you another time."

"Well, I mean, where?" Dammit. My skinny hero was brushing me off.

A shrug. "You'll see me." He started across the side street.

"I don't even know your name," I said.

"You don't need to," he called back. "I'll remember yours."

Black and White

Look more closely—you're missing
the mystery. My behavior
is no more my story
than a chalk outline on pavement.

If you were a cat, you would be
black and white, not entirely
unlucky, but suspicious anyway.
Not a loner, just alone.

Look more closely—I'm dressed
in bright red so I won't
disappear! Please confess
if you hear me or see me.

If you were a cat, you would
see through me, front to back,
my sighs and wonders. Black
and white, you would not run.

—Sandpiper Hollow Ragsdale

Chapter TWO

I write poems constantly. You know how some people cut themselves with knives or razors and say they do it because it's a relief to see the blood coming out? It's like an emotion they can *see* or something. I kind of get that—even though I hate to see my own blood—because I think I write poems for a similar reason. They spurt out of me, and then I feel better about myself. Like, thank God, at least I got *that* out. And I like the way they sound too, even though I don't always know what the hell they mean.

The night I met the Walker I wrote a poem called "Black and White." When I write, I let myself go into a space where somehow everything relates to everything else. It's hard to describe, but it's sort of like letting your eyes go out of focus, only you do it with your mind. Our black-and-white cat, Danny Boy, jumped up into the window seat with me and set the whole thing off. It's mysterious, really, how it happens.

I wanted to write a poem because I was feeling sort of bruised after the Walker left me behind. I mean, he wouldn't *allow* me to go with him. I couldn't figure out what I'd done to piss him off. Maybe I was talking too much about myself—I do that sometimes when I'm nervous—forget to ask about the other person. Then again, I usually think I'm more interesting than the other person. Anyway, a guy who won't even reveal his *name* to you is probably not going to fill you in on the rest of his autobiography.

There's a great place in the new house—Nathan's house, I mean—to hide out when I want to write. It's a window seat on the stair landing—there's a big curtain you can pull closed, and nobody ever thinks to look behind it. Even Daisy, my snoopy sister (named after the flowers my mother wore in her hair during her hippie wedding), hasn't discovered it yet. This house is so much bigger than our apartment was, I can actually have a complete thought without Colleen or Daisy interrupting me. I guess I have Nathan to thank for that. I guess I have Nathan to thank for everything now, which is getting really boring, and redundant too, since my mother and sister are falling all over him every single minute.

The two of them have been goofy with excitement all week about going to the airport to pick up Nathan and his daughter, Rachel. Rachel—she of the absolutely normal name—lives with her mother in San Francisco. We've never met her before. She just graduated from high school, which is why Nathan went out there, and now she's coming back here for five weeks—to be in the wedding, and then to stay with Daisy and me while the newlyweds are cavorting in Hawaii for ten days. She had better be extremely cool if she expects to live through ten days as my baby-sitter.

Apparently it's a big deal that she's coming. I guess there was a huge custody battle when Nathan and his first wife divorced, and Nathan lost big-time, which was pretty embarrassing since he's a shrink. He was allowed to see Rachel, but not very often, and she could never stay at his house because his ex-wife, Claire, said his new lifestyle was "too upsetting for a young girl to witness." His new lifestyle was nudism.

That was several lifestyles ago, thank God. Nathan says it was a "California midlife crisis." Also, he was thinner then. After he moved east and met my mother, they became a pathetically normal suburban couple you couldn't imagine having an interesting past. Now that they're headed for marital bliss, Rachel, Daisy, and I have the honor of being bridesmaids, whether we like it or not.

Daisy kept dancing in nervous circles and bumping into aggravated travelers trying to get to their gates. "I thought you said the plane landed already!"

"That's what the monitor said," Colleen told her. "It takes a few minutes to get everybody off."

"I wish they'd hurry up!"

"God, Daisy, do you have to go to the bathroom?" I said. She glared at me.

"Well, you're crashing into people. Can't you stand still?"

"No, I can't. Aren't you the slightest bit excited to meet Rachel? I mean, she's our new sister!"

"Stepsister."

"Still . . ."

"It won't be like having another sister, Daisy. She'll only be here for five weeks and then we'll probably never see her again. Besides, who needs *more* sisters? One is plenty, thank you very much."

"Well, see, I'm hoping this one might be *normal*."

"I think you're wrong about never seeing her," Colleen said. "Rachel has her own room in our house, just like you two. She can come and visit us anytime she wants to."

I crossed my arms and stared at her. "And you think she'll *want* to? After she *meets* us?"

Colleen is an expert at overlooking sarcasm. "I imagine she's happy to have a relationship with her father again, after all these years."

"Here they come!" Daisy shouted. "I can see Nathan! Whoa! Is that *her*?" Daisy turned to me. "She's beautiful!"

That is *so* like Daisy to immediately judge someone by the way she looks. We'd already seen Rachel's picture—we knew she was pretty. Although I'm not sure I knew she was *that* pretty. She was small, too. Short, thin, with long straight black hair that flew around her shoulders as she walked. Nathan pointed us out, and she smiled—a gigantic smile—as if she was delighted to be here, elated to meet her new *sisters*.

Colleen rushed up to them and kissed Rachel on the cheek even before she laid a wet one on Nathan. I don't think Rachel was expecting it, but she didn't flinch or anything. She looked like the kind of person who always knew what to do in any situation.

Nathan led her up to us. "Rachel, I'd like you to meet Daisy and Sandy Ragsdale."

"Sandpiper," I corrected him, just for the hell of it.

"Right." Nathan winked at me. He is *so* good-natured you want to barf. "And this is my daughter, Rachel." Nathan put his arm around his trophy child and presented her to us. Her small blue skirt ruffled over her knees, and the sleeves of her sweater fell just to the tips of her fingers. Perfect.

"I couldn't wait to meet you," Rachel said. It almost sounded like she meant it. "Dad has been talking about you two non-stop all week. I bet I know more about you than you know about me."

That was bound to be true. Nathan couldn't tell us much about his daughter because, until now, he didn't *know* too much. Claire had worked hard to keep them apart over the years, but now that Rachel was eighteen, she could do what she wanted. And I guess she wanted to see her father.

"We saw your picture!" Daisy gushed. "But you look even better in person!"

"Oh, thank you, Daisy! You're so sweet!"

I didn't have a saccharine compliment on the tip of my tongue, so I just said, "Hi."

"Hi, Sandy! Or do you go by Sandpiper?"

"Whatever." Suddenly both names sounded so stupid I couldn't bear it.

"I call her Sand*paper*," Daisy chimed in. "For obvious reasons."

Colleen wisely got between us before I could wring Daisy's neck. "Now that we're all together," she said, "it really seems like this wedding is going to happen, doesn't it?"

"I'm so glad you asked me to be in it," Rachel said. "It'll be so much fun."

"Sandpaper doesn't think so," Daisy butted in. "She's hardly doing anything to help us get ready. She didn't even want her name on the invitations!"

"Shut up, Daisy!" I said. Lord, she's such a baby! Sometimes she acts like she's seven instead of almost fourteen.

We took an escalator downstairs to get their luggage, and

15

I managed to fall to the back of the crowd so I didn't have to engage with Rachel immediately. I needed time to figure her out before I had an actual conversation with her. Daisy, of course, had already become her new best friend, jabbering away about God knows what. Meanwhile, Nathan fell in next to me and said something about being so proud of "my three beautiful girls." Lord. Like he thought I'd be jealous of Rachel or something. I have a father already, thank you very much.

The thing about the invitations is, Colleen thought all the kids should be listed on them as "announcing the marriage of our parents." It sounded ridiculous. I had nothing to do with these two people getting married, and I didn't want my name on the invitations. In the end, Nathan took my side, and they left the kids' names off. Rachel would probably thank me for this if she knew.

If anybody should be on the invitation as "announcing" Colleen and Nathan's marriage, it should probably be Rags, my dad. He's the one who introduced them to begin with, and then kept after Colleen until she went out with the guy. Not that Nathan is the first guy Dad tried to set Mom up with over the years. Not at all. He's been a regular dating service for her.

Rags and Colleen have a very friendly divorce. Oh, there was some yelling and crying originally. I was only eight, but you don't forget that stuff. Even at that age I didn't buy the reasons they were handing out—*grown apart, different goals,* blah, blah, blah. It took a while before I understood what the real problem was. Daisy and I met so many of Rags's new "girlfriends" those first few years, we couldn't keep them straight: Eve, Cindy, Kathy, Anita, another Cindy, Kristal, Marie, the list was endless. Finally I got it: Rags loved women.

Plural. Unfortunately, my mother was singular.

I'm sure Colleen was hurt at first, but the thing is, Rags still loved her, and I think since he didn't get married again, she felt like she was one up on all the other women. For the first few years she refused to go out with anybody. She was "through with men," all except Rags. When he came over to see Daisy and me, Colleen would hang around looking all sad, and I know for a fact they ended up back in the bedroom more than once while Daisy and I watched TV.

After a while I think Rags started feeling guilty that he'd ruined her or something, so he started fixing her up with guys he'd meet. I mean, really, he met some guy at a Home Depot once and decided he was perfect for Colleen, so he brought the guy over right *then*. He was really working at it.

But nobody made it to a second date until Nathan showed up last year with an armful of sunflowers. He wasn't the best-looking guy to come through the front door, but he wasn't putting on a big show to impress anybody either. You had the feeling the guy was really ready to fall in love with somebody, and I guess Colleen was ready too. In six months they were engaged.

Nathan's office is in Barlow, where Rags lives now, and apparently they met in a diner—they were both having lunch alone at the counter, and they hit it off. So Rags started telling Nathan about how great Colleen is, and how if he met her he'd really love her. Wouldn't you think a psychiatrist might have asked, *If she's so great, how come you divorced her?*

Anyway, Rags is going to be an usher at the wedding. Nathan considered asking him to be the best man, but my Grandma Edie (Colleen's mother) had a fit about it.

"Inappropriate" is Edie's favorite word, and she has had many chances to use it around this family.

While Nathan figured out how to get his bag and Rachel's three into the trunk, Daisy let Rachel in on the elaborate plans for the day.

"We have to pick out our dresses today, because it's already last minute if they have to do any alterations. Mom says we have to eat lunch first, but then we'll be all fat and none of the dresses will fit right, so I think we ought to go to the—"

"Lunch first," Colleen said flatly. "Nathan and Rachel have been on an airplane for six hours, and I'm sure they haven't had anything decent to eat." She turned to Rachel. "I'm sorry to have to rush you like this when you're probably exhausted from the trip, but we do have to get the dresses—"

"Don't worry about me," Rachel said. "I can't wait to try on dresses!"

"What size are you?" Daisy wanted to know.

"I'm a two petite."

"Me too!" Daisy shrieked, overcome by their similar tininess.

Dear Lord, I hated them both.

By the time Nathan dropped us off at Ceremonies, Adrienne, the maid of honor and my mother's best friend, was already there.

"Here you are!" Adrienne said, reaching to give Colleen a hug. "I was getting worried. I thought maybe the plane . . . or there was some problem with—"

"Everything's fine. Lunch took longer than we—"

"And *this* must be Rachel!" Adrienne said, beaming. "Oh,

what marvelous hair you have! *You'll* look lovely in lavender."

This was code for: Trouble Ahead. Lavender was Colleen's color of choice for the bridesmaids' dresses, but there had already been some rumblings from Adrienne, who was afraid the light color would make her look bigger than she already was. She was hoping to persuade Colleen that a darker purple would be just as nice, and maybe slice a few pounds off her hips too. I couldn't see what difference it made. At five-foot-ten, two hundred pounds, Adrienne wasn't going to convince anybody she was a size two petite. Besides, next to the toothpick twins, even I was going to look big, and I am a perfectly normal size ten.

The saleswoman who came over to help us took in the problem immediately. Here were two tiny girls, one tall girl with big boobs, and a middle-aged woman shaped like a grand piano, all of whom were supposed to be dressed in identical lavender gowns. Good luck.

There was one dress Colleen particularly loved, so obediently Daisy, Rachel, and I took our respective sizes into dressing rooms. They didn't have a size 22 for Adrienne to try on, but the saleswoman assured us that any dress we liked could be made up in any size. Adrienne sat on a big hassock, looking unhappy.

The dresses were made out of chiffon, and the skirts floated around us like lilac clouds. The tinies looked completely flat-chested in the low-cut bodice; I looked like I was offering my breasts to potential clients.

Colleen took one look. "Oh, dear, that really won't do." She glanced at Adrienne, and I knew she was thinking if the dress looked that slutty on me, what would it look like on *her?*

"Are you wearing a push-up bra?" Daisy asked me.

"*No.* This is what a female who eats looks like."

"I like this material," Rachel said diplomatically, flipping the breezy skirt around with her hands.

Daisy was still staring at my boobs like they were growing in front of her. "That's scary."

I crossed my arms over my breasts. "You're just jealous because you have the tits of a ten-year-old boy."

She laughed. "Right. I'd rather look like a milk cow!"

I slammed back inside my dressing room and pulled off the dress. There they were, two honeydew melons stuffed into a black bra, too damn big for the rest of my body. Even after two years it surprised me the way everybody noticed my boobs first, before they even looked at my face. Especially boys, of course. Even grown men would have to force themselves to look away, to meet my eyes. Sometimes I felt like screaming: *They're just mammary glands, you idiot! I didn't grow them for your viewing pleasure!*

Meanwhile, Colleen pillaged the racks. Adrienne squeezed herself into a size twenty purple silk dress that clung to her butt like paint. I tried on a dress that made me look like a very mature Little Miss Muffet. Rachel and Daisy tried on dresses that tripped them when they walked and padded their non-existent shoulders into wings.

When the dressing rooms were piled with discards and Adrienne was near tears with frustration, the saleswoman came up with another idea.

"You know, these days wedding parties don't all have to wear identical dresses. Why don't we try something? Line up the way you'll be walking down the aisle."

We lined up in order of height: Daisy first, then Rachel, me, and Adrienne.

Colleen looked us over, and her eyes got caught on the top of my head. "Gosh," she said, "I always forget how tall you are! You got that height from Rags."

"You *forgot* how tall I am?"

"You could be your father's twin if you were a boy. And your hair was longer," she said, laughing and brushing my unevenly shorn hair with the palm of her hand.

"And you were old," Daisy added.

"What do you mean, you *forgot*?" I think what really bothered me was how quick Colleen always is to disown me. All my life she's been telling me I'm just like Rags. Which is okay. I used to be thrilled that I was more like him than like Mom and Daisy. But sometimes I feel like the two of them have drawn a circle around themselves and I'm on the outside. Or maybe it's just that Rags doesn't want me in *his* circle anymore either.

"Oh, don't get all upset, now. You know what I mean. I don't think about your height until I see you next to someone short." Colleen put one arm around Rachel and one around Daisy, just in case I didn't know who she meant.

The saleswoman was ignoring our chatter, running around the shop, gathering things off the rack "You will love this idea," she assured us. Her solution was to have Daisy in a lavender silk; Rachel in a slightly darker silk; me, another shade darker; and finally, Adrienne in a purple silk suit with a long jacket that covered her hips. The dresses were all different, but using the same fabric and the shades of lavender tied them together. We were never going to do better.

While Carol was getting our measurements—we'd been there so long we were on a first-name basis now—I started thinking what this wedding would really be like. Colleen in a beautiful white dress, doing it right this time. Everybody in fancy clothes, stalking through Nathan's landscaped garden holding wineglasses. A band. A tent. A cake that cost more than a plane ticket to Moscow. Enough food to feed a hundred refugees for a month.

Was this the same woman who scandalized her mother by marrying Rags on a beach at 5 A.M. without telling anybody? Their favorite story used to be about how they exchanged their vows barefooted just as the sun was coming up. I kept thinking that was the *real* Colleen. All this ritualistic crap must be what Nathan wanted. After all, he's a doctor—people like that always want to show off any chance they get. Colleen would have gotten married in a red caftan again, wouldn't she?

By the time we walked out of Ceremonies, it was almost seven o'clock.

"Should we stop for dinner before I drive you home?" Adrienne asked. "I'm starving."

Even I could see that Rachel was starting to stagger.

"Thanks, honey," Colleen said, "but I think we better call it a night. Rachel has been up since all hours. You must be wiped out, aren't you?"

Rachel smiled. "Getting a little tired." She turned and looked up one side of the street and then down the other. "I'm just starting to realize I'm on the East Coast. I've never been here before."

"Is it different from California?" Daisy asked.

"Well, this town is. I mean, the buildings are older, and the streets are narrower. Yeah, it seems very different."

"But do you like it?" Daisy insisted.

Rachel smiled. "I think I *will* like it. I like *you*."

Daisy turned happily red. So, everyone I lived with was crazy about someone else I lived with. Except, of course, me.

Dresses

Hundreds of dresses are singing
in falsetto voices, trying to get my attention.
I'm drowning in silk, or would be
without my unsinkable breasts.

The bride will be bound and gagged
by tradition. At her first wedding she wore
cotton with daisies. This time she's pinning
her hopes on white lace, pearl buttons.

Daughters should be smaller than
their mothers. They feel smaller anyway.
They should wear lavender dresses
and wind themselves around her body like wisteria.

—*Sandpiper Hollow Ragsdale*

Chapter **THREE**

Monday was the beginning of exam week at the high school. I had spent the weekend with my newly expanded family, feigning enthusiasm for details of the big shindig (flower arrangements, musical interludes, cake decorations— Lord, what a waste of mental energy a wedding is), and had not cracked a book until Sunday night. Actually this was no big deal since I was coasting through high school anyway. At least that's what my guidance counselor said. He wanted me to take honors courses so I'd have no time for life. Screw that. Besides, then I'd have classes with all those young geniuses. *Boring.*

Daisy's eighth-grade graduation was the week before, so she was available to keep Rachel entertained while Colleen and Nathan were at work. No hardship for her. Colleen drove Nathan to work so Rachel could use his car and take Daisy to the mall. Daisy, fast food, and hideous clothing—lucky Rachel.

I had only one exam Monday—American history—and it was over by eleven o'clock, so I walked downtown, figuring

I'd bump into somebody I knew. Hammond is a small town, and it's all built around the harbor. That's where most of the stores are too, so everybody ends up down there eventually.

The somebody I was hoping to run into, of course, was the Walker. I'd seen him around the used bookstore before, and once heading up the hill past the galleries. I figured I'd get lunch at Mama June's Deli, which has big windows on Front Street, so I could watch for him without being too obvious.

I'd already ordered a tuna fish sandwich and picked a lemonade out of the refrigerator when I saw Andrew come in the door, followed by Derek and this other guy they call Hamilton, which I think is his last name. Hamilton looks dumber than the other two combined, which is quite a feat.

I kept my back turned to them, but Andrew saw me right away. "Hey, guys, look! There's a Bitchburger at the counter. I love Bitchburger, don't you? Anybody want a bite?"

I kept my mouth shut for a change and paid the woman behind the counter. She gave me a funny look, like I had my underwear on over my clothes. I felt like saying, *Don't look at me! They're the assholes!*

"Yeah," the Hamilton ignoramus said, "I've heard about the Bitchburger."

But it was Derek who came up to me, pretending to be friendly. "Hey, Sandy. How you doing?"

"I was fine until you showed up."

"I heard you got a new boyfriend. Or is that over already? I know you don't like to stick with one guy too long."

I ignored him and took my sandwich to a little table near the window. There was a second chair at the table, and Derek plopped himself down in it. The other two stood behind him like Secret Service agents, their hands on their hips.

"Do you mind?" I said. "I don't want to talk to you, Derek. Or your stupid friends either."

"Don't be that way, Sandy." He smiled his one-sided smile that I never trusted for one minute, ever. "I thought we were old friends."

"Why'd you think that?" I took a bite of sandwich and tried to look out the window past the guards.

"Well, you know. Because you gave me blow jobs for two weeks." He said it loud enough for the counterwoman to hear him. I could see the disgusted look on her face as she flung her sponge into the sink and walked into the back room.

The sandwich stuck in my throat, but I took a big drink of lemonade and managed to swallow it. The Three Stooges were high-fiving and laughing at me.

"Leave me alone, you vermin."

"Here's the thing, Sandy. You know, me and Andrew had our shot at you . . . so to speak. . . ." They collapsed in laughter again. I wrapped my sandwich in a napkin and stuffed it into my purse. I didn't have to sit there and listen to this shit.

But they followed me out the door, Derek pulling on my sleeve.

"Let go of me," I said.

"Come on, Sandy, do you think it's fair that you did us and not Ham? We're a trio, you know? Brothers. We look out for each other." He was grinning like a monkey. How could I ever have liked this person?

"You're out of your mind."

His phony smile collapsed into a scowl, and all of a sudden I thought he might actually hit me or something. "I don't think I'm the crazy one here, Slutster," he growled.

I turned away to cross the street, but he grabbed hold of my backpack. "Don't run away from me, Sandy. We're having a conversation." Hamilton and Andrew were outside now too, and the three of them were just about surrounding me when I heard a car horn honk. The first thing I thought was, *It's the Walker*, which was ridiculous, of course, because he won't even get *in* a car. I guess I sort of believed all that superhero stuff I made up.

Rags was getting out of his vintage Mustang by the time I turned around. "Is there a problem here, Sandpiper?"

I glared at Derek. "Not really."

"Why don't I give you a ride home?" Rags said. Rags hadn't been my hero for a few years now, but in an emergency, you take what's available.

"Sure." I hiked up my backpack and kicked Derek in the shin as I walked by him.

"Who's that?" Hamilton asked his cohorts. "Is that old guy her boyfriend?"

"Her dad," Derek mumbled, giving his friend a punch in retaliation for the kick I'd given him. They walked off down the street, but Derek looked back, angry. Why the hell was he so mad? I'd stayed with him longer than Andrew.

I decided I better deflect any questions Rags might have, so as soon as I crawled into the front seat, I said, "You're not teaching on Mondays this semester?"

"Classes were over at Peckham three weeks ago. Colleges are on a different schedule—you know that."

"Oh, right. So how come you're in Hammond?"

I knew from the look on his face I shouldn't have asked. A

woman, no doubt about it. He was seeing somebody in town and, for some reason, didn't want to admit it. Finally he came up with an excuse. "Needed new boots. You know I always come back to Randolph's to get my work boots."

I nodded. Yeah, a playwright needs a good pair of work boots. No evidence of a shoebox in the backseat. I guess a playwright keeps his work boots in the trunk. Gimme a break.

We were almost back to the house before Rags said another word—which is not unusual these days. Looking at us now, you'd never guess Rags and I used to be best buddies. I mean, we actually liked hanging out together—sometimes we'd go fishing, sometimes he'd take me to a pool hall, sometimes we'd drive to this all-you-can-eat place on the highway and pig out on biscuits and baked beans, which we both love. If we ran into somebody he knew, he'd always say, "Have you met my colleague, Dr. Sandpiper, the eminent philosopher?" And I'd shake the person's hand. He always had great stories to tell too. He made me laugh like nobody else could.

But the last couple of years all that changed. I guess, in a way, it was my fault, but there's nothing I could do about it. What happened was, I hit puberty and Rags went into shock. Like, overnight I got these giant gazongas. I remember the day Rags first noticed; it was terrible. He looked at me the same way other men were starting to, except he also looked like somebody had just kicked him in the balls. I guess I looked too much like the people he was dating. Is that *my* fault? I put on bulky sweaters, but it didn't help. Our great relationship was history—my boobs had scared the crap out of him. These days he acts like I'm some acquaintance whose presence makes him vaguely uncomfortable.

Most of the time this attitude makes me want to scream, but right then I wasn't in the mood to talk to him anyway. I hated to admit it, but it shook me up a little bit the way Derek and his pals were acting. When I'm finished with a guy, I'm usually very good at avoiding him. Nobody has ever come after me like this. Not that there have been *that* many. Eight or ten. Maybe more.

I guess that sounds like a lot of guys to be with before you're even sixteen. Maybe it is too many. I get caught up with guys when they say they like me so much, that they *need* me. Derek really liked me—at least, he acted that way. I liked him too at first, but it lasted only a few weeks before he was getting on my nerves. And once I break it off with a guy, I don't even want to see him anymore. For a while I feel like I don't want to see *any* guys anymore, but that doesn't last long either. I don't know what I want.

Finally, Rags cleared his throat and said, "So what was that all about? With those guys?" But he said it like he'd really rather not know.

"Just some kids from school."

"It looked like they were kind of . . . harassing you or something."

"I can handle them."

Rags gave me a startled look. "I don't want you to have to *handle them*, Sandpiper. Boys can be . . . well, they can be—"

"Yeah, I know, Dad."

"No, I don't think you do know." Rags sat up straight and tried to look parental, but imparting wisdom makes him squirm. "You can't always trust boys. Some guys will take advantage . . . and I didn't like the way those boys were acting.

Almost as if they were threatening you—"

"They weren't. They're a bunch of idiots is all. Don't worry about it."

He didn't say anything then until we pulled into Nathan's driveway, but I could practically hear him thinking. I tried to jump out of the car fast, but I didn't make it. He had one hand on my arm, while the other raked through his hair.

"Sandpiper, I think I should have talked to you more about these things. About boys . . . and how to . . ." He grimaced. "Well . . . protect yourself."

"Dad, I'm way past you here."

His eyes got wide. "What do you mean?"

Oops. "I mean, you know . . . sex ed and everything. I know all about it." I smiled at him, all innocence. At the same time I was glad he wasn't catching on, I was also thinking, *How stupid are you? You, my own father, look at me and think, "Sex."*

"Oh, yeah, sure. But still—"

He was interrupted, thank God, by Nathan's car pulling in beside him, Rachel at the wheel. Daisy jumped out of the passenger seat and ripped Rags's door open.

"Hi, Dad! Come meet Rachel! She's awesome!"

Rags stood up in time to see the black hair flying around the front of the sedan, the big dark eyes above a pale pink smile, tan legs in short shorts. His look of polite interest changed to one of serious appreciation before my eyes. Disgusting.

"See you later, Dad," I said, heading for the house at a gallop.

"Okay, kiddo." Why was I not surprised? That fast he'd forgotten about the threat to my life, sidetracked by Rachel's limbs.

* * *

An afternoon at the mall had completely bonded my sister and stepsister-to-be. At the dinner table Nathan was beside himself with glee, promising them credit card usage, rights to his car, whatever seemed necessary to keep the love flowing.

Daisy was expounding on how Rachel had helped her buy the *perfect* pair of jeans. "Even the clerk in the store said I'd never find a better fit."

"Yeah, and clerks are known for their objectivity," I said.

"And we got the most adorable earrings to wear with our bridesmaid dresses, Mom. You'll love them."

"We almost got two more pairs, but I was afraid Sandpiper and Adrienne might not like them," Rachel said, glancing at me sideways.

Gee, what were the chances of that? "The dresses aren't even alike," I said. "Why would we wear matching earrings?"

"I agree," Rachel said, heartily nodding her head, like, we were *so* on the same page here.

"Did you eat lunch at the food court?" Colleen asked, all excited, as if they'd gone to *Paris* for the day.

Daisy nodded and giggled.

Rachel gave her a conspiratorial look. "Do they know about Sam?" she asked.

Daisy blushed.

Mom cocked her head. "Sam? Who's Sam?"

"My . . . boyfriend," Daisy said.

"What? Since when do you have a boyfriend?" Mom asked, but she looked elated at the news.

"He's *very* sweet," Rachel assured us. "Just a doll of a kid. He ate lunch with us in the food court." She winked at Daisy.

"Can he come to the wedding?" Daisy said. *"Please?"*

"Wait a minute," Mom said, laughing. "I didn't even know you *had* a boyfriend. When did this start?"

"Five minutes ago," I said. "Daisy, the wedding is three weeks from now. At your age going with somebody lasts about three days."

Daisy glared at me. "Oh? How long does it last at *your* age?"

Nathan leaned over the table to pet Daisy on the head. How can she *stand* that? "Well, Daisy, I think we might like to meet this boy sometime. And then assuming he's as nice as Rachel says, why not invite him? The more the merrier!"

"Thank you, Nathan!" Daisy jumped up from the table.

"Where are you going?" Mom asked.

"To call Sam. To see if he can come over and meet you!"

Oh, they all loved that, hoo-hoo, hee-hee, what an adorable child she is.

I was not about to stick around the house for the presentation of some smelly eighth grader. Colleen asked me to load the dishwasher, while Rachel helped Daisy pick out the perfect T-shirt to go with her perfect new jeans. I was rushing, and banging things around a little bit.

"Sandpiper, slow down. You're throwing silverware on the floor."

"Sorry. I'm in a hurry."

"Are you going somewhere? I was hoping we all could do something together tonight."

"Mom! I've been hanging out here all weekend. I need to . . . to go to the library. It's exam week, you know."

"Oh, sure. I'm sorry, honey. I'm so involved with this wedding thing. . . . It's just that I'd like you to get to know

Rachel a little better. She and Daisy seem to be crazy about each other already."

"Do I have to be *crazy* about her? She's fine. I just don't think she's going to be my best friend, you know?"

Colleen chewed on her lips while she swirled the sponge around the frying pan. I knew there was something else on her mind, and I was hoping to get out the door before she managed to figure out how to say it. I almost made it.

"I was just wondering," she blurted out as I was drying my hands on the dish towel, "what happened to Melissa and Allie? I haven't seen them around here for ages. You guys used to be so close."

"Can we talk about this later?" I said, sighing.

"Did you have an argument or something?"

"No! It's just . . . we don't have that much in common anymore. They have boyfriends, and they're busy."

She looked grief-stricken, as if I'd just told her they were hospitalized with yellow fever. "Well, but if you aren't hanging around with Melissa and Allie, who *are* your friends now? You never bring anybody home anymore."

I hated to be put on the spot like that. My hands got all itchy, and I felt like I was about to implode. "Okay, okay. I'll bring somebody home sometime."

She put her hand on my shoulder. "Do *you* have a boyfriend, honey?"

"Mom!" I shrugged away from her.

"You used to talk to me about everything. Now I don't even know who your friends are!" Her eyes welled up. "Is it because I'm getting married again? I thought you liked Nathan."

God, I'd never get out of there. "I like Nathan *fine*." I'd
like him even finer if he wasn't so damn nice every minute, but
I didn't tell her that. I scratched at the palms of my hands with
my nails. "And no, I don't have a boyfriend. I'll tell you when
I do, but now I *really* need to go. . . ."

She wiped a hand quickly across her cheeks and waved me
away. "Okay. I know you're busy, honey. I'm just crazy these
days. Do you want me to drive you to the library?"

"No! I mean, you have to stay here to meet Sam, don't
you? Besides, it's nice out. I feel like walking."

I dashed upstairs to get a camouflage notebook, but I was
a little too slow getting back down. The front doorbell rang
just as I got there.

"Hi! I'm Sam!" the short kid with the red forelock
announced, sticking out his hand. "Who are you?"

I beckoned him in, then slipped out the door around him.
"I'm the one they don't talk about." I said, and disappeared
into the darkness.

Warning

A storm brews,
clouds threaten rain, then
lightning is your final
warning: get inside, go
to the cellar, wait
for better weather.

But how long do you have to
wait? What if better weather
is a myth? Maybe the climate's
changed forever, and you'll have to
spend your last days waiting
for the water to cover your head.

A storm brews,
clouds threaten rain,
but I'm not waiting around
for a final warning. I'll meet
the threat, that thundering
bully, under the unruly sky.

—*Sandpiper Hollow Ragsdale*

Chapter FOUR

I knew I'd find the Walker that night—I just knew
it. I walked through Blessingame Park first, but the only people
there were two mothers pushing strollers and a jogger who was
about ready to drown in his own sweat. *So* attractive. Then I
hit the back roads up the hill to the cemetery, figuring I'd scan
the town from up there, look for that old beat-up jacket of his.
What do you know, there he was right in the cemetery, actually
sitting down for a change, on top of a tall, wide stone.

He jumped a little when I came up behind him.

"Waiting for somebody?" I asked.

"Oh, it's you," he said. "No, I'm just watching the sun go
down."

"I've never seen you when you weren't walking."

"This time of the day I let myself rest a little. I sit here with
my friend Calvin," he said, patting the stone.

CALVIN HILLENBRAND, 1958–1994.

DEVOTED HUSBAND AND FATHER.

"You always sit on this same stone? Doesn't anybody
mind?"

"Not so far. Me and Cal talk. He's a good guy." the Walker kept his eyes on the horizon so he wouldn't miss a minute of sunset.

"Do you . . . I mean, did you know this guy?"

He shook his head.

I looked at the dates again. "He was only about thirty-five when he died."

"Thirty-six," the Walker said.

"He must have had kids—it says he was a devoted father. That's sad. If he really *was* a devoted father."

"Even if he wasn't, it's still sad."

"I guess."

It seemed like the Walker really wanted to concentrate on that sunset, so I wandered a little distance away and leaned on another stone, *Helen Steiner, 1902-1986.* Somebody who'd had a good long life. Well, long anyway.

It was one of those nights when the sky gets all streaky with orange, and the sun is radioactively red. From the cemetery you can look down over the sailboats in the harbor and all the old houses along Front Street with gardens full of tall flowers just coming out. Hammond seemed really pretty from up there, like a town anybody would love to live in. From a distance you couldn't see each individual jerk who made your life suck.

Even after the sun went below the horizon, there was still enough reflected light to see by. The Walker stood up and stretched.

"Finished talking to Cal?" I asked.

"Yeah, we had a heart-to-heart. Like always."

"Where are you going now?"

"Walking."

"Well, I figured that. Where?"

He shrugged. "I never know till I get there."

"Don't you ever go home? You do live somewhere, don't you?"

He looked away from me and started walking before he answered. "I live somewhere."

I scrambled down the hill, trying to keep up. "In Hammond?"

He nodded.

"Where in Hammond?"

He hesitated a minute but then said, "In back of the Thai Seasons restaurant. An apartment."

"Do your parents—"

He stopped at the bottom of the hill and faced me, looking slightly annoyed. "Sandpiper! Do I ask you a million questions?"

"No, but you could if you wanted to. And by the way, thanks for remembering my stupid name. Are you going to tell me yours?"

He sighed. "Look, if you want to walk with me a little while, it's fine, but no more questions. Okay?"

"*Okay!*" Jeez, they were just normal questions. No doubt in my mind—this guy was hiding stuff. Like why wasn't he in school? Did he have a job? Didn't his parents care that he spent so much time wandering around? Why wouldn't he tell me his name? I could think of a dozen more questions I wanted to ask.

Instead I walked next to him in silence as he headed down an alley that led to Weewinnet Beach. Hammond's harbor is like a large oval, open at one end, and there are lots of small secluded beaches, especially at this end of town where the harbor opens to the ocean. Weewinnet used to be my favorite beach when I was little. Colleen and Daisy always preferred Moss Beach, which is bigger and has bathrooms, an ice cream stand, and a huge social scene in the summertime. But Rags would often bring me to Weewinnet on a Sunday afternoon. So we could build sandcastles in peace, he said, without somebody's Frisbee or dog landing in the middle of it. Weewinnet is a small beach, and it disappears completely at high tide, but it has the best view, especially if you'd rather look out at the wide ocean instead of rich people's boats.

At the end of the alley the Walker picked up the trail down to the beach, and I followed.

"I used to come here all the time," I said. "Mostly with my dad."

"You did? I didn't think anybody came to Weewinnet."

"Not too many. How do you know about it?"

A shrug. "I have maps."

"You're kind of an explorer, aren't you? I mean, you're not just walking; you're looking for things."

He didn't answer right away, and it was getting too dark for me to see his face very well. "You could say that, I guess. I've found some good shells on this beach, deepwater shells that get stuck here when the tide goes out." As soon as we got to the sand, he padded along the shoreline, bending down now and then to look more closely.

"I've never found anything but regular old mussel and clam shells along here," I said. "Maybe some periwinkles in a tidepool."

"You weren't really looking then."

Honestly, he could be so condescending. Was I crazy to be following this weirdo around in the dark? A weirdo who didn't seem to give a damn about me, who wouldn't even tell me his name! Of course, the alternative was going home and hanging out with Daisy's new boyfriend and the flawless stepsister.

"Ah-ha!"

Weewinnet is protected from the lights of town, so I could barely see where the Walker was anymore. But then I felt him nearby, and it made me shiver.

"Look at this! Can you see it?" He was holding my hand and carefully putting something into my cupped palm. "It's a duckfoot!"

My hand opened. *"A duck's foot!"*

He grabbed my hand. "Not a duck's foot. Duckfoot. It's a shell. Look at it."

When I held my hand close to my face, I could make it out. Sure enough. It was a small whorled shell, maybe two inches long, with a large opening that fanned out like a wing.

"You just found this?"

"I've found them here before. They aren't that unusual. This looks like a perfect one though—not chipped or any- thing."

"Wow. I wish I could see it in the light."

"Take it home. You can have it."

It wasn't like he'd given me some big gift. It was a stupid shell, and he'd found lots of them before. So I didn't want to make a big deal out of it, but really I was so happy to have that shell.

"Thanks," was all I said.

* * *

We stood there silently for a while, watching the moonshine ripple on the incoming tide. It reminded me of how Melissa and Allie and I used to be, years ago. We could hang out all afternoon sometimes and barely talk—it was comfortable just being together, reading or watching a movie. I didn't really understand what had happened to our friendship any more than my mother did. It was like that Robert Frost poem: they took one road, and I took the other.

Of course, there was one big way in which hanging around with the Walker, especially in the dark like that, was completely different from being with Melissa and Allie. Not just because he was a boy, but because he was such an *unreachable* boy. Usually if I was in the dark with a guy, I could feel the power I had over him, and it was exciting. I knew I could start a chain reaction with a single touch. Not this time though. This time *he* was the one who had the power—I didn't dare touch him. My nerve endings felt as frayed as the cord on the old lamp Nathan made us throw out when we moved in with him. He'd called it a fire hazard, which is how I felt—ready to burst into flames.

The Walker wasn't one to stick around in one place, so before too long we were back on the path to the alley. "Won't your parents be worried about you? It's dark out," he said.

No kidding. "They think I'm at the library studying."

"That's probably a better way to spend your time than following me around."

"I'm not *following* you. Are you trying to get rid of me?"

"No, I'm just saying I'm not much fun to hang with. Maybe you figured that out already."

"I figured out the Walker is not the Talker, if that's what you mean."

We were back under streetlights by then, and I could see the corners of his mouth turn up. Oh, God, I'd made him smile again!

"I go to the library," he said, "first thing in the morning, when the only other people there are old guys reading newspapers."

"So you don't walk all the time."

"Nope. Sometimes I sit down and read."

"And sometimes you sit on Calvin Hillenbrand and watch the sun go down."

"Yeah, some life." And then he seemed to leave again; he stared down the road, his eyes dark and shuttered like an abandoned house.

For a second I felt scared. Maybe I didn't want to know the Walker's secrets. Maybe we should all keep our lousy secrets locked up in dark rooms where they can't hurt anybody else.

"I should get back home. They'll never believe I could study this long."

He nodded. "Okay."

"Thanks for the shell."

He started down the road, his shoulders hunched up in leather. I missed him already.

"I'll see you later," I called after him.

"Maybe so."

I didn't know why I liked the Walker, but I did. It wasn't that he was so very good-looking, although I did kind of like his too-long hair and the way his wrists hung out of the small jacket and made his hands seem large. And I loved the way his smiles came from far away and really *meant* something. He was serious in a way other guys I knew weren't. On the other hand, I had the feeling if I never saw him again, he wouldn't care at all. It seemed like I hadn't scratched his surface even the littlest bit. And I wanted to. Very much.

Why did it matter? When I thought about it, none of my boyfriends had ever scratched my surface either. I never even thought of them as *boyfriends*. Well, the first guy, Tony, I guess I thought of him that way. Allie certainly did. She was so jealous I couldn't believe it. But by the next week she was going with Tony's best friend, and all was forgiven.

The weird thing is, she's still going with Tony's best friend. They act like they're married—at sixteen. Ugh. At least Melissa went with a bunch of different guys before sticking with Billy English all year.

What kills me is how they look down on me now. I know they do—I can feel it. All the excuses about why they don't have time to hang with me are bullshit. The last conversation I had with them, Melissa said, all seriously, "Sandy, can't you see that these guys are just using you?"

"Is that an exact quote from your mother?" I asked.

"We're just trying to help you," Allie said. "Don't you want a *real* boyfriend?"

"Maybe I don't," I said. "And anyway, how did you two get to be born-again virgins?"

Haven't talked to them much since then. Of course, this happened before I was down to the Andrews and the Dereks. Their advice doesn't seem quite as stupid now, although they still need to figure out how to say stuff like that without sounding like God's newest angels.

Duckfoot

Shell with an angel wing, yellow
on the outside, pure white
inside, a weatherless tornado,
churning and hollow.

Boy with a leather jacket, quiet
on the outside, turbulent
inside. Sometimes his black eyes
churn; sometimes they're hollow.

Girl with an attitude, fearless
on the outside, paralyzed
inside. Her perfect shell covers
a churning heart, a hollow hell.

—*Sandpiper Hollow Ragsdale*

Chapter FIVE

My last exam was English on Thursday morning.

It was the only class I actually enjoyed, which is mostly because of Mrs. Humphries who is way too smart to be teaching high school. If I ever became a decent student, it would be because of somebody like her. Even her exams are creative. My favorite question on this exam was, "If you were Walt Whitman, what would you sing about?" (He has this great poem called "I Sing the Body Electric.")

We didn't have to answer the question with a poem, but I did. Mrs. Humphries appreciates my poems, the ones she's seen anyway. Unlike Mr. Todd, the emperor of the high school literary magazine, who thinks I write "filth." And this is based on two lousy poems I turned in last year, one that used the word *crap* and another that used *vagina*! I'm guessing he's not a big Walt Whitman fan either.

When the final bell rang, I was finishing my last stanza.

"Are you almost done, Sandpiper?" Mrs. Humphries asked.

"Yup. Just about."

I was the last person left in class, but Mrs. H. didn't rush me. She sat down and started looking over some of the tests that had already been turned in.

"The last question was fun," I said when I handed her my paper.

She laughed. "Somehow I think you're the only student who thought so! You know, you really ought to consider taking the honors English class next year. You've done so well in here."

Time to disappoint someone else. "The thing is, Mrs. Humphries, I do well in here because I like the stuff you make us read and how you talk about it. If I didn't, I'd be doing lousy. So I'm only doing well because of you."

She looked surprised by that. "Well, I'm flattered, but, you know, Ms. Eldred is teaching the junior honors course next year, and I think you'd like her. She writes poetry too."

I was pretty skeptical, but I told her I'd think about it over the summer. I felt kind of sad saying good-bye to her—almost the way I used to in grade school when I'd fall madly in love with my teacher every year and then leave in tears on the last day of school. I mean, I wasn't weeping over Mrs. Humphries, but I'd miss her.

I'd already cleaned everything out of my locker, so there was nothing to do but walk home, which seemed sort of anticlimactic. Wasn't I supposed to be dancing around in circles with my friends? *Yeah, school's out! It's summer! Let's play!* If I had any friends to play with.

Through the big glass lobby doors I could see three girls standing around talking in front of the school—Melissa and Allie with Meryl McKee. A little spark of happiness flared up in me, but then I remembered, and I stamped it out. Melissa and Allie don't *approve* of me. I'm not good enough for them anymore.

They saw me walk out the door and pasted fake smiles on their faces. I'd almost rather they just ignored me altogether.

"Hi!" Melissa said. "Did you just finish a test?"

I nodded. "English. Mrs. Humphries."

"God," Allie said, "can you believe our sophomore year is over already?"

"Not too soon for me," I said.

Meryl McKee took a step backward. She probably didn't want anyone to think she was actually conversing with a bad influence such as me. Meryl is barfingly perfect: always gets As and keeps her skinny legs glued together like Popsicle sticks.

"Do you have plans for the summer?" Melissa asked me. How bizarre that she had to ask, that we hadn't planned out the whole hot season like every other year. Even last summer was good—Allie was AWOL with Peter, but neither Melissa nor I had any boys hanging around to screw things up (for a change) and it was almost like old times.

I shrugged. "I guess I'll see if I can get a job—you know— after my mother's wedding is over."

Melissa and Allie exchanged quick looks. "Right!" Allie said. "That should be fun!" Both of them grinned maniacally.

Lord, I was going into shock from the sugar overload. If people don't like you anymore, they ought to just act like it. It doesn't make you feel any better when they carry on like long-lost assholes.

"I have to go," Meryl said. "Tennis lesson."

Melissa and Allie started making noises about how busy they were too. Like I might think they had time to hang out with me, for God's sake. I headed off down the sidewalk. They were my old life—no sense looking back.

Still, the idea of being replaced by Meryl McKee was aggravating. At least I had a sense of humor. Meryl was as much fun as poison ivy. How could Melissa and Allie prefer her to me? Was it because Meryl was such a *good girl*, and they were the newly appointed sex police?

God, Allie and I had been friends since the fourth grade, and Melissa and I had been friends since we were five or six— ever since our disastrous year of dancing lessons with Miss Patsy. Our clumsiness had bonded us. We spent so much time together that our mothers got to be friends too.

Which made me wonder if Colleen had invited the Renfrows to the wedding. That would be awkward. She and Nathan kept inviting more and more people to this thing—it was becoming the social event of the summer. They were having it in Nathan's—or rather, *our*—backyard because there was room for a million people back there. The whole thing seemed to me like it was getting a little bit out of hand.

Every day Colleen got more and more anxious about pulling it off, so I wasn't too surprised when I got home to find her sitting at the dining room table with Grandma Edie and Adrienne, making more lists.

"How come you're home already?" I asked her.

"George sent me home because I was making so many mistakes—I put the wrong swirls on top of a whole tray of chocolates."

"She put the orange swirl on the raspberry truffles,"

Grandma Edie said. "I'd certainly be upset if I got one of those. Orange is my favorite."

Mom sighed. "I can't seem to concentrate these days."

"I don't know why you don't just quit and be done with it," Adrienne said. "If I was marrying somebody who made a good living like Nathan, I'd run out of my kindergarten classroom so fast—"

"*Kindergarten!*" Edie shuddered at the thought of it.

Colleen just smiled. She liked dipping chocolates. It was a good job for her—she used to love painting, but now she was happy dripping milk chocolate on her clothes instead of burnt siena. And she got to bring the mistakes home for us, so Daisy and I thought it was the best job a mother could have. She ate them too, but never seemed to gain a pound.

Meanwhile, the half-empty Sweet Tooth candy box sat in the middle of the table, taunting the rest of us. Adrienne reached for a cashew turtle, my favorite.

"Let's stop the eating now and start getting this straightened out," Grandma Edie said. She's a very no-nonsense person, which makes you wonder how Colleen ended up so sappy. I think my mother works hard *not* to be like her own mother.

"For example," Edie continued, "don't your friends know the proper way to send back an RSVP, Colleen? It's as if they can't be bothered to make up their minds one way or the other. Look at this one: the card asks them to pick chicken or fish for dinner, and she writes down, *Either one.* Who would answer an RSVP like that? You don't ask the host to make your choice for you!"

Colleen glanced over at the card. "Oh, that's from Sylvia at work. I'm sure she really *doesn't* care. Put her down for chicken."

"And this one!" Grandma continued to rant. "You've invited the whole family, and they answer saying, *At least two. Not sure about Melissa.* Well, *make* sure about Melissa! What is wrong with these people? Can't they make a decision?"

Melissa? That card had to be from the Renfrows, which answered my question. They'd been invited, but Melissa obviously didn't want to be caught dead over here.

"Edie, it's not that big a deal," Adrienne said, reaching for the Sweet Tooth box again. "They'll rent a few extra tables and chairs just in case."

My grandmother pursed her lips and narrowed her eyes. Uh-oh. "Well, Adrienne, excuse me for saying so, but obviously *you* have no idea what it's like to plan a wedding. I'm sure it doesn't seem like a big deal to *you.*"

Oh, Lord. Edie really could be a bitch sometimes. I didn't dare look at Adrienne, but I knew what was coming. She cleared her throat, sniffed, and then ran for the bathroom, slamming the door behind her.

"Mother! What is wrong with you! That was a terrible thing to say to Adrienne."

Grandma didn't even look guilty. "Oh, she's always been so sensitive."

"Well, if you know she's sensitive, why do you—?"

"If she'd stop wolfing down the chocolates, maybe some man would look at her!"

"That's enough!" Colleen said. "Adrienne is my best friend, and I won't have you talking about her like that!"

Edie stood up from the table, ramrod straight. You can never get away with telling Edie she did something wrong.

"Fine. You and Adrienne can sit here and try to figure out how many of these rude guests are coming. I have better things to do with my time."

She grabbed her raincoat off the back of the couch and headed for the door, but by this time Colleen's need to smooth everything over had switched back on.

"Mother, don't be mad."

"I'm not mad. I'm just not staying in a place I'm not needed."

Colleen followed her outside for a minute, but Edie stalked off. There was something about Grandma Edie I really admired, although I certainly tried to avoid ever having her anger focused on me. She was like a little rat terrier; her bark was bad and her bite hurt too, but it was fun to watch her run around scaring everybody.

Colleen leaned against the wall. "I should go talk to Adrienne, but I just don't have the energy. Why did I ever think having a wedding would be fun?"

"Got me. It's not on my top ten list."

She shook her head. "Adrienne must be so upset. Of all the things to say to her. Your grandmother certainly knows where to stick the pins."

"You'd think Adrienne would be used to Edie by now," I said. "She's known her forever."

"Since we were twelve years old. Still, you never get used to meanness if you aren't that way yourself."

I did a little math in my head. "God, you've been friends with Adrienne for more than thirty years!"

She smiled a little. "I can hardly believe it myself."

"Did you ever get mad at each other?"

"Of course we did. You can't be friends with somebody for

that long without getting on each other's nerves now and then." She gave me a suspicious look. "By the way, why isn't Melissa coming to the wedding with her parents?"

I shrugged, not too happy with the direction in which the conversation was suddenly headed. "It didn't say she definitely wasn't coming."

"Sandpiper, I know something has happened between you and Melissa and Allie. Why won't you talk to me about it?"

This called for a giant sigh as I fell onto the couch. "It's just one of those things that happens. We hang with different people now."

"Well, you must be pretty *unfriendly* if she won't even come to my wedding."

"Maybe she has other plans that day!"

Now it was Colleen's turn to sigh. "Is it because I'm getting married to Nathan?"

"Mom, Melissa doesn't even know Nathan."

"No, I mean *you*. Is that why you've been so distant lately? Nathan tries so hard; I keep thinking you'll change your mind about him."

I concentrated on untying my sneakers. "I have no problem with Nathan. He's fine. You can marry anybody you want to."

"Well, of course I can, but . . ." She sank onto the edge of a nearby chair and ran her hand through her hair. "Sandpiper, there's something we need to discuss. I talked to your father last night. He called to tell me he thought you might be running with a tough group of boys."

I laughed. "*Running?* With *tough boys?* I don't know what Dad thinks he saw, but I'm not *running* with anybody. I was talking to a couple of guys, that's all. They aren't even my friends. God!"

"He's worried about you, honey. That's all."

I sat up straight and threw down a shoe so hard it bounced. "Well, if he's so damn worried, why the hell can't he talk to me himself? Why does he tell you to do it?"

"Calm down. He said he tried to talk to you, but, well, it's hard for him. You're a teenaged girl, and he's . . . he's—"

"He's too busy with his girlfriends to deal with me."

Colleen's face got all soft and sad. "Oh, honey. Your father adores you—you know that."

"Right." I stood up and collected my wayward shoes.

"Is that what's eating you? Your dad's not around enough?"

"Did you know he was seeing somebody in Hammond now? That's where he was when he saw me *running around with boys* the other day."

Colleen twisted her weighty engagement ring around her finger. "I did actually. He asked if he could bring her to the wedding."

"What?"

"Your grandmother will have a fit, but I know the woman, so I couldn't really refuse him. Laura King. She works at the library. She's very nice."

"He's bringing a *date* to your wedding?"

"Oh, Sandpiper, don't make a big deal of it. You know how Rags is—he's always got to have a woman on his arm."

"How long has he been seeing her?"

She sighed. "Well, a little longer than usual, I suppose. Six or seven months now. But I don't think it's serious."

I stared at her. My mouth was still open when Adrienne

wandered slowly into the room, her eyes red, but dry.

"What's going on?" she asked.

Colleen popped up and ran to her. "Edie's gone. I'm sorry, Adrienne—you know how she can be. She said to tell you she apologizes."

Disgusting. "Mom, would you please stop trying to make everything all right? You're *lying*. Edie would never apologize to Adrienne or to anybody else. And if he's been with her that long, Dad *is* serious about this Laura King person. And the truth is, he can't stand to be around me anymore! That's just the terrible truth! If I can face it, why can't you?" And then I ran upstairs before they could see that facing the truth had beaten the crap out of me.

I Sing the Body Chaotic
(with apologies to Walt Whitman)

I sing the body chaotic,
broadcasting its need to touch and be
touched, afterward
shutting down all communications—
longing always for the impossible—
to find beneath the passion and desire,
a heart.

I sing the body emotional,
the center that no one sees,
which might be the thing we call soul
but is probably less mysterious
than we wish, is probably just my chemicals
reacting to your chemicals,
not poetry.

I sing the body confusing,
the flesh, muscle, fat, and blood
in which I live, electrified, naked
meat unable to escape the pleasures
or the demands of this liquid
prison I swim in as in
a sea.

O, my body! No longer that of a child,
sheltered and loved, now you show yourself off,
the breasts large, the hips wide, the voice
whispering, the sex laughing.
I use you, but I do not understand you.
Are you heart, soul, sea, chemicals,
or poetry?

—*Sandpiper Hollow Ragsdale*

Chapter **SIX**

Now that school was out it was harder to avoid

Rachel. I was having a noontime breakfast of frozen waffles
when she came into the kitchen. "Hey!" she said.

"Hey yourself."

"You finally got up, huh?"

"Gimme a break. I just finished school."

She laughed. "My friends all sleep late too, but for some
reason I just can't. As soon as the sun comes up, I'm awake. So
I just get up."

"Sucks for you," I said.

Her smile faded, and she opened the refrigerator door to
search for yogurt, her primary food group.

I decided it might not kill me to try a little harder. "I was
thinking maybe we could go down to the beach today, if you
want to."

Rachel bounced back. "Really? I haven't been to the beach
here yet. It was chilly this week, but it's warm today."

"Yeah. We can go to Moss Beach. That's where most
people go."

"Now? Right away?"

God, she was so happy it made me feel bad for ignoring her all this time. Obviously, the kid was desperate for a little excitement. After our nourishing snacks, we suited up. I was glad to see she'd put a T-shirt and shorts on over her suit—it meant there'd be that much less time that I'd have to compare her half-naked body to mine. I got the towels and sunscreen and stuck them in a canvas bag along with a few bottles of water and my notebook. Rachel put in some magazines too.

Our beach chairs were in the basement where we'd stuck them when we moved in the previous month. I hosed them off before sticking them in the trunk. There was no question of walking the half-mile to Moss lugging all this stuff since Rachel obviously *owned* Nathan's car these days.

She jumped into the driver's seat and revved it up. "This will be so much fun. Thanks for asking me."

"Don't you go to the beach in California?" I asked.

"Once in a while but, you know, we live right in the city, not on the water. Besides, I don't have much free time when I'm home." She popped one of Nathan's tapes in the player: the soundtrack from *The Big Chill*. She shrugged. "Better than nothing."

"So, what would you be doing if you were home?" I realized she'd been living with us for almost a week already, and I hadn't asked her anything at all about her life in California. Bad stepsister.

"Mostly working. I wait tables at a place called Lulu's. It's really popular—people have to make reservations weeks ahead. Normally they don't hire people who haven't waited before, but my mother is friends with the owner so he trained me. I've worked there for two years, part-time during the school year, of course. The tips are fantastic.

"Then during the summer I'm a volunteer tutor three days a week for a group called Kathy's Kids. I *love* that. We work with elementary school kids, helping them get their reading skills up to grade level. Some of them are *so* adorable I just want to take them home with me!"

I should have guessed she'd be one of those do-gooder types. That bright smile, those shiny eyes. She should have been wearing a pin that said, I TRY HARDER!

"Doesn't leave you much time for fun, does it? Working that much?"

"Sure! A lot of my friends do Kathy's Kids too, so we're together then, and I don't work at the restaurant every night. Do I look like an all-work-and-no-play type?"

I shrugged. "Do you have a boyfriend?"

"Sort of. Jeff and I have been together for a while now."

"Why do you say 'sort of'?"

"You know. He's going to college in Colorado, and I'll be at San Francisco State. Too hard to do a long-distance relationship. We've discussed it and decided we should see other people. We're too young to make a commitment anyway."

For an eighteen-year-old she sure had life all figured out. Make money, help the needy, go to college, eat your yogurt, wait for marriage, keep the parents happy. Were people born knowing how to be perfect?

"What about you?" Rachel asked as she turned the car into the Moss Beach parking lot. "Do you have a boyfriend?"

I considered my answer as I climbed out and locked the door. *Not really, but I have been blowing several guys lately.*

"I guess I'm between boys at the moment," I told her. I hoisted the canvas bag onto my shoulder, and Rachel took a beach chair in each hand.

She looked interested. "You guess?"

"I mean, I'm definitely done with the last one, but the guy I'm interested in now, well, we're just friends."

She nodded. "That's how the best relationships start, I think. As *just friends*."

The beach was so crowded we had to walk single-file between all the blankets and towels. I should have figured it would be like this, the first really hot day of the year with school just over. Lord. There were a bunch of kids from my class all gathered around a big cooler, blaring a radio. Why hadn't it occurred to me that all these idiots would be here?

I led Rachel in the opposite direction from my classmates, and we waited for a mother to load twins into an enormous stroller so we could have the spot she was vacating. Not bad. It was in front of some big boulders, which would keep us from being too noticeable.

Before flopping into her beach chair, Rachel stripped off her outer layer. A simple, tiny red bikini covered the important areas. The rest of her was polished by a deep, unlined tan. She bent over the canvas bag so that her hair swept the sand and her butt attracted the attention of every male on the beach, and pulled out the sunscreen.

"Would you do my back and then I'll do yours?" she said, handing me the bottle.

I took off my shorts and shirt. I might not wear a size two petite and have movie-star hair, but my body attracted attention too. I adjusted my top for maximum exposure before I started oiling Rachel up.

When she turned around to do my back, she immediately complimented my suit, which made me realize how ragged it was, worn thin by all the boogie boarding Melissa and I had done last summer. Hard to believe that had been only a year ago.

We'd just settled into our chairs when I saw Derek and his posse walking toward us, kicking up sand. Please! Who would have expected those deviants to show up at the beach?

"Hey, look guys, Sandy's here!" Derek announced.

I kept my eyes on the ocean, but Rachel whipped off her sunglasses to get a better look.

Derek noticed. "I don't think I know your friend, do I, Sandy?" Andrew was staring stupidly at my boobs, snapping his gum, but Hamilton had his eyes focused on Rachel. He probably thought she was a mirage.

"I'm Rachel," she chirped, giving the boys a big smile.

"Nice to meet you, Rachel. I'm Derek. These jerks are Andrew and Hamilton."

The jerks nodded.

"Are you Sandpiper's friends from school?" Rachel guessed.

"Yeah, yeah, we've known Sandy a long time. We know her *really* well," Derek said.

"Yeah, *really* well," repeated the brain-dead Andrew. Hamilton just stared.

Crap and double crap. How was I going to explain this to Rachel? She was looking at me, waiting, I suppose, for me to say just where it was I knew these fine gentlemen from, and how it happened that we were such close friends.

"I don't recall seeing you at the high school," Derek the Suave said. "Are you new here?"

"I'm visiting from San Francisco." Rachel glanced at me as though asking permission to tell, and then said, "Actually, my father is marrying Sandpiper's mother in a few weeks. I'm here for the wedding."

Andrew hooted, but Derek kept up his act. "Isn't that wonderful? Sandpiper has such a lovely family."

That did it. "You don't even know my family, Derek, so just shut up and leave us alone."

Rachel looked at me, alarmed, then pulled her knees up to her chest and hugged them. She shut up, but Derek didn't know how.

"What do you mean? I know that cute little sister of yours. *Daisy.* We can't *wait* for her to show up at the high school next year. And now we find out you've got a gorgeous stepsister too. What a family, huh, guys?"

More grunts from the monkeys.

Rachel stood up and gave Derek a look that clearly said she'd gotten his number. "I'm going in the water, Sandpiper. You coming?"

"In a minute."

Andrew and Hamilton watched her wade daintily into the surf, then dive under the surface and disappear. Disappointed, they turned back to me.

"Listen, Derek, you better shut up about Daisy. She's just a kid. She doesn't . . . do stuff . . . like I do."

"Really? You mean sluts don't run in the family? How about that one?" He jerked his thumb over his shoulder.

"What's *wrong* with you? Why can't you just leave me alone?"

Derek sat down in the beach chair Rachel had just left. "The thing is, Sandy, nobody likes to be dumped. I'm not good enough for you. Andrew's not good enough. You don't seem too interested in old Ham here. That hurts our feelings."

"Screw you." I leaped out of my chair. "I never want to see any of you again. *Leave me alone!*"

The two lummoxes tried to imitate Derek's sneer, but they just looked like they had toothaches. I walked down to the water without looking back, then waded in up to my shoulders even though the breaking waves froze me solid.

What was I supposed to do? Were these creeps seriously dangerous or just really annoying? I wished there was somebody I could talk to about this, but there wasn't. Certainly not Colleen—not two weeks before the wedding of the century. And Rags would pass out before I even got to the gory details. Rachel wasn't likely to enjoy the story much—it wasn't the kind you could read to Kathy's Kids. Melissa and Allie would have been the obvious candidates if they hadn't disappeared from my life.

When I finally turned around again, the terrible trio was leaving the beach. It was over, for now, anyway. Probably they just wanted to scare me. Well, the hell with that. I wasn't going to let a bunch of stupid punks push me around. And they better not try anything with Daisy either.

God, it was freezing in that water. Surely Rachel must have gotten out by now, but when I looked back at our chairs they were empty. It would be just my luck if she drowned—for the rest of my life I'd be known as the girl who killed her step-sister.

I shivered my way back to shore before I spotted Rachel a hundred yards down the beach. She was talking to one of those guys who have muscles on their muscles. I guess he was one hilarious dude because Rachel couldn't seem to stop laughing at everything he said. Finally she turned around and saw me watching her.

"Sandpiper!" she called, waving to me. "Come here!"

Oh, Lord. Why had I ever come up with this beach idea? Why didn't I just ask her to go to a movie, where it's dark?

She started talking before I even got to them. "You won't believe this. It's so funny!" she said. "This is Mark Conrad."

Mark had his shaking hand ready. "Hi. You're the almost stepsister," he said.

"Yeah." His hand engulfed mine as he yanked my arm from its socket.

"This is so amazing," Rachel said. "First of all, I practically crashed head on into Mark while I was swimming, and then once we realized we hadn't killed each other, we started talking. He asked me where I was from . . ."

"I couldn't believe she was from San Francisco. I go to college right near there . . ."

"Well, in Santa Cruz, but it's not that far. Isn't that a coincidence?"

"And I go up to San Francisco all the time . . ."

"And he's even been to Lulu's!"

"Wow." What else could you say about a head-on coincidence like that? I didn't remember ever seeing the guy around town before so I asked him if he lived in Hammond.

"I didn't grow up here. My mother moved here after my parents divorced, and I'm spending the summer with her."

Sometimes it seemed like everybody's parents were divorced. What was the point of getting married anyway? The wedding was a big pain in the ass, and then the divorce was a bigger pain in the ass. In between you might have a few kids who, if you were lucky, would only be pains in the neck.

I had the feeling I was interrupting Rachel's flirtation, so after a minute or two I walked back to our chairs. I'd brought along my notebook to work on a poem, but I wasn't in the mood after my run-in with those jerks, so I just pulled out Rachel's magazines: *People*, *Ms.*, and *Vogue*. Was that multiple personalities or what? In one you had Julia Roberts cavorting on the beach and "Di's Boys: Cuter Than Ever!" In the next there was an article on *Roe v. Wade* and "Women Who Make a Difference." And finally the magazine that stank of perfume and advertised six-hundred-dollar shoes announced, "Green Is the New Black!" Who *was* this Rachel person?

Nothing else to do so I looked through the *Ms.* cover article. I hoped *Roe v. Wade* wasn't overturned, but if it was, at least my promiscuousness wasn't going to get me pregnant. I wasn't *that* stupid. On the other hand, hoovering those hoodlums hadn't exactly been the act of a genius. What would *Ms.* magazine say? That I should enjoy my female sexuality? Unfortunately the whole on-your-knees experience had never left me feeling very liberated.

By the time Rachel returned, I'd dropped the magazines in the sand and nodded off.

"Sorry I was gone so long," she said, sitting down beside me. "Mark is really nice."

"Umm." Nothing like sleeping outside in the sun to turn you into a zombie. I licked my lips. "You gonna see him again?"

"Actually I am. He's taking me out for dinner tonight!"

I opened my eyes. "That was fast."

She shrugged. "What can I say? We hit it off."

Something told me Rachel often hit it off with guys.

"I guess it's bye-bye to old Jeff."

"Not necessarily. I mean, I like them both. It wouldn't be the first time—"

"What? That you've had two boyfriends at the same time?" I sat up to look at her.

She nodded. "It's like insurance. I know that sounds bad. I guess I'm one of those girls who hates to be without a boyfriend. Is that awful?"

"I'm no expert on good behavior," I assured her, as I rubbed my fingers over my cheek. "We should probably go. I think my face is baked."

"Didn't you put sunscreen on it?"

"Forgot."

Rachel examined my nose. "Yup, you're burned. Let's get out of the sun." She picked up her magazines, brushed them off, and stowed them in the bag. I struggled to my feet, feeling sweaty and dizzy. Rachel clicked the beach chairs closed and we headed for the parking lot, me staggering behind her through the sand.

"Sandpiper," she said, "who were those guys? Derek and whoever. They seemed really weird to me."

"Yeah, they are. I was . . . friends with them for a while, but I'm not anymore. They're losers."

"They're sort of scary."

"Not really. Just jerks." I hoped it was true.

"Well, I'm glad you're not friends with them anymore."

When we got back to Nathan's car, there was a flyer under the windshield. At least that's what I thought it was, or I would have grabbed it first. Rachel pulled it out while I was stashing the chairs in the trunk.

When I came around the car, she had a funny look on her face. "I think this is from them," she said, handing it to me.

It was a piece of paper torn out of my notebook—they'd gone through my notebook! Lord! The note was scrawled in a felt-tip pen: *You ought to be a little kinder to your old friends, Sandy. I bet your sister Daisy is friendlier than you are. Think it over.*

Derek must have written it—I doubted the other two could spell "friendlier." But how did he know what car to put it on? Had they been following me? I balled the paper up and stuck it in the pocket of my shorts.

"Are you going to tell me what this is all about?" Rachel asked.

"What what's about?"

"Come on, Sandpiper. I won't tell them."

"Tell who?"

She slapped the hood of the car impatiently. "Your mother, my father, anybody!"

Just then I saw him: the Walker, heading up Front Street in his leather jacket—in this weather! Could I talk to *him*?

He turned up Wardwell Road; he'd be out of sight in a minute. I grabbed my flip-flops from the beach bag as I threw it into the backseat. I was putting them on as I ran, yelling back to Rachel at the same time.

"Sorry! I really have to go . . . do something. I'll be home soon, okay?"

"Where are you going? You aren't going after those guys, are you?"

"No. I promise. It's all cool. Don't worry."

"Be careful! How will you get home?"

I was half a block away already, but I yelled back to her, "Two feet. It's called walking."

The Almost Stepsister

Six months ago I didn't know
you existed. Why, at sixteen,
would I want another sibling?
The one I have is thief enough,
making off with everything
from new shoes to motherly
affection. And neither of us
needs the example of you,
a girl with two parents
crazy for her attention.

Maybe growing up without a pesty
brother or sister, you think you've missed
something. Pillow fights or dinner
table tricks. Sister secrets.
You'd like to tell me how you keep
your tan so dark and smooth, how you keep
men's eyes glued to your red bikini
and then your needy mouth.

But what do I have to share with you, my
out-of-the-blue stepsister?
Would you like advice on ditching lowlife
scum? I know what drinks will mask
the bleachy taste of cum, but no,
I doubt you itch to know the details
of my sketchy life. Still, I'll admit,
you could be worse. You could be the person
I long to become.

—*Sandpiper Hollow Ragsdale*

Chapter SEVEN

"Hey!" I called after him as I sprinted up Front Street. It was ridiculous not knowing his name. "Leather jacket guy! Wait up!"

I rounded the corner on Wardwell, and he was standing right there, waiting.

"Leather jacket guy?" he said, almost smiling.

I was panting from my hundred-yard dash. "Well, you won't tell me your name—I have to call you something."

"I thought you said people call me the Walker?"

I banged sand out of my flip-flops. "So I should yell, '*The!* Oh, *The!*'"

That did make him smile. "I see the problem. How about if you just call me Walker? That's a name, right?"

I tilted my head sideways, flirting a little. "It's not *your* name though, is it?"

He shrugged. "Maybe it will be someday. I'm thinking of changing my name."

"From what?" I asked innocently.

"Clever girl," he said. "Let's walk—my feet get itchy standing still."

I plodded up Wardwell next to him. My shoes weren't made for hiking, but I kept up.

"Maybe I should change my name too," I said.

"You know, I was thinking about that."

"You were?" He was thinking about *my name*? When I wasn't even around?

"I was thinking that Sandpiper is too odd, and Sandy is too common—you need a distinctive name, but not a weird one. Piper would be good, I think. It suits you."

I didn't know what to say. He'd been thinking about me.

"You don't like it?" he said.

"No, I do like it. Piper. Because I'm always piping up, you mean?"

A light laugh. "Well, that too, I guess. I was just thinking a piper is a musician, like the Pied Piper."

"Oh, that's a problem—I can barely whistle. I don't think I could get anybody to follow me out of town. But yeah, call me Piper. Walker and Piper. I like it."

He didn't respond to my linking up our names like that. Flirtation didn't really seem to have much effect on him. So how was I supposed to connect with him anyway?

We were walking uphill when I suddenly realized how thirsty I was. *Burning* with thirst.

"Can we stop at that convenience store?" I asked Walker. "I really need some water."

Without answering, he crossed the street and we headed inside, where of course I realized I didn't have a nickel on me.

"Lord, I don't have my wallet. Could I borrow some—"

"I'll get it." He picked up two bottles of water and paid for them.

"I'm sorry. I didn't mean for you to have to—"

"I'm not poverty stricken, you know. I can buy you a bottle of water."

I unscrewed the cap and gulped down several swigs. "Do you work?"

He sighed. "More questions. Yes, I work."

"When? You're always walking around."

"I stock shelves overnight at Walgreens, okay? Midnight to six. Perfect job for an insomniac."

We went back outside and continued walking, but he was ignoring me now. It certainly didn't take much to piss him off. Which pissed *me* off.

"How should I know if you're poverty stricken or an insomniac or any other damn thing? You act like it's a crime for me to know anything about you! For instance, why do you wear that hot jacket even in this heat? You're always wearing that jacket!"

I figured he was going to keep ignoring me, but I stuck with him anyway. We walked at least two blocks, past the fitness center and a Chinese restaurant, before he said another word.

"I'll tell you about the jacket if you really want to know."

"Of course I want to know. Why else would I ask you?"

He kept walking and didn't look at me. "It belonged to my father. He died when I was seven. I started wearing it way back then because it smelled like him. It was too big for me then, and I guess it's too small for me now, but I'll never get rid of it. It's all I have left of him."

Well, that'll teach me to be such a nosy brat, huh? I mean, who expects an answer like that to *Why do you wear that hot jacket all the time?* I didn't know what to say. I didn't know anybody who'd lost a parent. I mean, in a way you lose them in a divorce, but it's not like death.

I opened my mouth a couple of times, but the right words weren't there, so I closed it again. We kept walking; he seemed calmer than before.

"Hey, smell that?" Walker said, sniffing. "There's honeysuckle around here somewhere. Down here, I think."

He headed down a narrow side street, and I followed. Sure enough, there was a long hedge of honeysuckle full of blooms.

I took a deep breath of the sweet smell. "You could smell this from up on Wardwell?"

"It's what I do. See, hear, smell, touch, sometimes even taste. When you spend a lot of time walking around outside, you notice things differently." He reached through the fence behind the honeysuckle and picked something that looked to me like a weed. He crushed it between his fingers and held it out to me.

"Here's something you can smell and taste."

I took it from him and sniffed hesitantly. "Oh, I should know what this is."

"Mint. You can eat it too."

"No thanks. What if a dog peed on it?" I picked a honeysuckle blossom instead and pulled out the honey tube to suck. "I'm sorry I asked about the coat," I said. "It wasn't any of my business."

He shrugged. "It's okay. I haven't talked about it in ages. It doesn't hurt to talk about it. Anymore."

"Do you remember your dad?"

He picked a blossom and swirled it between his fingers. "Not too much. My mom used to tell me stuff, so I'm not sure now what's a memory and what's a story."

"How did he die? Or shouldn't I ask?"

"Cancer. He was sick for about two years before he died, but I guess I didn't really understand what was going on. I'm the youngest."

"So, you have brothers and sisters?"

Walker's face tightened, and he suddenly looked right into my eyes. "You're good, Piper. I'm talking more than I meant to."

"All I asked was—"

"I have one sister. She's eight years older than I am. That's all I'm telling you about my family, okay? Enough."

"*Okay!*" I chugged some more water out of my bottle as we continued down the alleyway. If he wouldn't talk about himself, maybe he'd be willing to dissect *my* life, if I actually had the nerve to tell him about it. "So, I need some advice. That's why I chased after you. I have this problem, and I can't really tell anybody about it."

"Then why tell me?" He was still mad, I guess, that I'd gotten that information about his sister out of him.

"Maybe because you don't really know me very well, so you won't get all crazy about it like my family would. And also, it seems like . . . you think about things."

I could tell he was loosening up again. "Everybody thinks about things, Piper."

I *loved* being called Piper. "Not necessarily. Some people just have an immediate reaction, and then maybe later they think about it, but by then it's too late because they already said something awful and they can't take it back."

He stopped walking and turned to look at me as if I'd just announced the secret of life on earth.

"What's wrong?" I asked.

"Nothing. Just . . . you're right about how people react."

"So, can I tell you about this . . . problem?"

"Okay, I guess." We walked on.

"Well, see, there are these guys. Three guys, actually, and they've been, I guess you could say, harassing me." How much detail would I actually have to confess?

"Is one of them the guy I saw you with last week?"

"Yeah, that's Andrew. But he's not the worst. Derek is the worst. He's been sort of scaring me lately. Although maybe it's not a big deal. Maybe I'm just—"

"What's he done?"

"Well, see, he's mad at me because . . . well, he's just mad at me. And now he's saying that he's going to get back at me; he's threatening to do something to my younger sister, Daisy."

"What did you do to this guy?"

"*Nothing!* I sort of went out with him, that's all. And then we broke up, and he's all mad about it."

"Derek? I thought you were dumping Andrew when I saw you the other day."

"I was. It's complicated." I stopped walking and he did too.

"Obviously, but I can't give you advice unless you tell me the whole story."

I groaned.

"You don't have to tell me if you don't want to. I respect that."

"No, I want to. It's just that . . . you'll think I'm a slut. Everybody else does."

He shrugged. "Well, then one more won't matter."

I studied his face. "Was that a joke?"

He smiled one of those faraway smiles. "Yeah."

"Lord, how am I supposed to tell with you? You only make one joke a week."

The smile faded, but slowly. "Really, Piper, I won't judge you. Whatever you did, it's in the past."

"Could we go up to the cemetery and sit on Simon what's-his-name for a while? I don't know if I can walk and tell it at the same time."

"Okay."

"Oh, Lord! Simon's not your father, is he?"

"I thought we were through talking about my family?"

"I'm sorry. We are. I just suddenly thought, maybe . . ."

"No, Simon was the same age as my dad when he died, so I like to talk to him, that's all."

We walked silently along the sidewalks of Hammond, finishing our water, passing a few dog walkers and an old man with a cane, but nobody I knew. Walker smiled at people and some of them said hello to him. Probably they recognized him because he walked through their neighborhood so much.

The cemetery is the highest point in Hammond, and my flip-flops were having a hard time with the rocky path you have to climb to go in the back way. Without saying anything, Walker took my hand and pulled me up over the rough parts. I would have kept holding on, but as soon as we were on the gravel path, he let go. Simon was still there, waiting for us.

"You can sit on Simon's headstone, since you're doing the

talking," Walker said. "Maybe he'll have better advice for you than I will." He settled himself on the grass in front of the grave.

I couldn't figure out how to start telling the story. Why was I telling a guy I liked about my crappy past?

"So, why do people think you're a slut, and what does that have to do with the three guys you're afraid of?" Walker's dark eyes looked straight into mine.

Okay, get right to the point. "The thing is, I guess I'm kind of a serial dater. I mean, I never stay with one guy for very long. Like, sometimes just a few days."

"And that makes you a slut?"

"*No.* It's what I do with them . . ." Lord, this was embarrassing.

"You have sex with them?"

"No! Well, not really sex." I put my head down and my hands up over my face. "I mean, I guess I'm the queen of . . . blow jobs."

Walker didn't respond, and I peeked out between my fingers.

"Go ahead," he said, looking not at all shocked.

My hands flopped to my lap. "I've never had *real* sex with anybody! But I guess I have a reputation or something now. Like guys know about it, and some of them . . . you know . . . want it. Ugh. I don't know why I'm telling you this. I'm sorry. It's awful. I don't even know why I *do* it!"

"You don't want to do it?"

"Not really. I did for a while, but I don't anymore—I just don't know how to stop. Everybody thinks this is who I am— I guess it is who I am, but I'm sick of that person. How can I suddenly be somebody else?"

He nodded and thought for a minute; then he said, "It seems to me you already *are* a different person, or you wouldn't have told me."

I sighed. "Well, if I've changed, you're the only one who knows it."

A shrug. "Gotta start somewhere. Do you think these guys would really hurt somebody—your sister or you?"

"I don't know. They're creeps. Especially Derek."

"I guess you can't tell your parents."

I shook my head. "My mother is getting married in two weeks—she's already a wreck. And my father would totally freak out on me. I have to handle it myself."

"Yeah, you do," he said, looking discouraged. "But I think you have to tell your sister so she knows to stay away from them. How old is she?"

"Thirteen. God, she'll hate me."

"She might not understand it right away, but you're protecting her by telling her. Maybe they'll forget about it after a while. You know, guys sometimes do crazy things, especially guys that age."

I grunted. "Guys that age? Like you're so much older?"

"Yeah, I am so much older. Believe me."

"Derek is seventeen—you're eighteen!"

He was staring at me, all intense again. "I'm saying, you never know what people will do!"

"Okay, I know. You look like you're mad at me now. Is it because of what I told you?"

"I'm not mad at you."

"You look that way. Will you still walk with me now that I told you about . . . what I've done?"

He made a motion as if shooing away a bug. "Piper, don't be silly. It's not as if you hurt anybody, except maybe yourself. These guys are using you—you know that, right? You have to stop doing it. You're worth more than that." He touched my nose lightly. "Now go home and put some aloe on your nose before it peels off."

I nodded because I was afraid if I tried to speak I'd start to cry. Here was a person who knew how to say it right: *Take care of yourself, Piper. You're worth something.*

Summer and All
(with apologies to William Carlos Williams)

By the road to the old cemetery
under the first hot sun of the season,
not a breeze to cool a red cheek
and three more months to burn,

you smelled the honeysuckle and the
mint, put them in my hand. I tasted
the honey. You listened.

All along the road we saw flowers fully
open, at the peak of their once-a-year
performance, alive as they would ever be,
the green grass assuming it would live forever.

Such a change came over me
on the road to the old cemetery.
Summer became a golden promise, a lovely
liar, or a chance for new life.

—Piper Ragsdale

Chapter EIGHT

Walking home, I decided that no matter what his secrets were, Walker was the coolest guy I had ever met. Which meant I suddenly had a huge crush on him, which hadn't happened to me since I first met Tony Phillips in the eighth grade. Of course, the situation was somewhat complicated by my recent confession. And further complicated because now I wanted to be with *him* in the way he'd just told me I was worth more than. I hope this doesn't mean I'm an incorrigible sexual pervert.

I was trying to sort through all these feelings when I opened the door onto yet another wedding disaster. Adrienne was standing in the middle of the living room holding out her purple wedding suit to my mother, whose mouth was hanging open so far her jaw looked unhinged.

"I'll pay for the dress, Colleen; don't worry about that," Adrienne was saying. "You can have it cut down to fit somebody else. Hell, it's big enough to fit *two* other people."

"I can't believe you're saying this!" Colleen said. "*Now!* Two weeks before the wedding!"

"Colleen, I'm so sorry." Tears were dripping from Adrienne's chin. "I hope you'll be able to forgive me someday. I just can't do it."

Rachel and Daisy were huddled on the stairs, listening. I tiptoed over to them. "What's going on?"

"Adrienne just told Mom she doesn't want to be in the wedding," Daisy whispered. "She looks too fat in the dress."

"And she doesn't have a date either," Rachel said.

"So? Who has a date?"

"I do," Daisy said. "Dad does. Rachel does."

"You *do*?" I glared at Rachel.

She smiled apologetically. "Well, not yet. But your mother said I could invite Mark if I want to. You know, the guy on the beach."

"Right." So, now that Adrienne was backing out, I'd be the only dateless bridesmaid in the lineup. Whoopee.

"Don't you think you're being a little selfish?" Colleen said. "This is my *wedding*, Adrienne. You're my maid of honor!"

"I know." Adrienne let the dress fall onto the couch so she could fish a tissue from her purse.

"Where do you think I'm going to get another maid of honor *now*? My *other* best friend?"

"You have another one?" Adrienne looked up.

"Of course not!"

Adrienne sighed heavily. "Maybe you could promote one of the girls to maid of honor."

Colleen sank back into a chair. "Why are you doing this, Adrienne? Is this about what Edie said to you last week? Because you *know* how my mother is—she's always saying something tactless and awful. You've been around her enough years now. . . ."

"It's not that. Not only that. I know you can't understand, Colleen. You've never had to look in the mirror and wonder who that sausage-shaped woman is looking back at you. Just the thought of walking down the aisle behind those three beautiful young girls . . . And I've never even met the best man—he's going to fly in from California, take one look at me, turn right around, and fly back. I'm sorry, Colleen. I just can't do it."

Colleen was quiet for a minute, looking down at the new Oriental rug she and Nathan had bought a few weeks ago. When she looked up again, her face was white. "Is there any way I can change your mind? I *want* you standing next to me."

That was too much for Adrienne. Her face wadded up like Play-Doh. "I want to be there, Colleen, I *do!* But I can't! I just can't!" The tears were spurting as she turned around and ran for the front door, tripping just slightly on the hem of her long skirt, cursing herself, then disappearing down the sidewalk.

We waited until Adrienne's car pulled away to go into the living room.

"Wow," Daisy said, "I can't believe she did that."

Colleen didn't respond—she was back to carpet watching.

"Maybe she'll change her mind," Rachel said.

Colleen shook her head. "I can't believe it. She's been my best friend my whole life. How could she do something like this to me on my wedding day?"

It seemed like Adrienne needed somebody on her side. "Mom, think about it from her point of view. . . ."

She was in no mood for that. "*Her* point of view! It's an honor to stand up for someone at their wedding! I'm her best friend!"

"Yeah, but maybe she's thinking about how she probably won't ever have a wedding where *you* can be the maid of honor. Besides, she already did it for you once, didn't she?"

Colleen looked startled.

"Did she?" Daisy asked. "Was Adrienne your maid of honor when you married Dad?"

"Well, I guess she was. I mean, it wasn't a real wedding like this one. But she did stand up for me. She and Rags's brother Peter were the only witnesses we had. And now I'm remembering that Peter made some stupid remark about her size, which she overheard. Is that what this is about?"

"I don't know, but making her do it twice is a little bit like rubbing it in her face, isn't it?" I said.

"Oh, Sandpiper, you make me sound awful! I just want her there beside me!"

I shrugged. "I know. I'm just saying . . . I can see why she might not want to."

Daisy plopped down on the arm of Colleen's chair. "Well, I can't. Who cares if she has a date or not? And everybody knows she's fat—it's not like she looks worse in this dress than in anything else!"

"God, Daisy, are you turning into Grandma Edie, or what?" I said.

Colleen stood up and pushed us aside. "That's enough now. I'm going upstairs to think about this. And I don't want any of you, *Daisy*, bad-mouthing Adrienne."

"I'm not . . ."

"Enough!" Mom headed up the stairs while Daisy pouted.

The minute the bedroom door closed, Daisy said, "Like we don't all know she's fat."

"So she's fat! Is that a crime!"

"Guys," Rachel said quietly, "your mom will hear you."

I glared at Daisy, thinking about how impossible it was going to be to talk to her about Derek, to tell her *my* secrets. What if she went running to Colleen and told her? That's all Mom needed right now. Still, I knew Walker was right—I had to tell her.

Rachel went up to her room to get ready for her dinner with Mark. Nathan wasn't due home for another hour. There wasn't going to be a better time.

Daisy had retreated to the kitchen to make herself a cup of cocoa. I watched her stirring the powder into the hot water.

"Is there enough hot water for me to have tea?"

"Think so."

I shook the kettle and got out my favorite cup. Daisy picked up her cocoa and started to leave.

"Could we talk a minute?"

"Why? So you can yell at me some more?"

"I'm not going to yell. There's something I need to tell you about."

Daisy looked surprised. "What? You never tell me anything!"

"Just sit down a minute, would you?"

She looked suspicious, but she brought her cocoa over to the counter and perched on a high stool. "So?"

How in the hell was I supposed to do this? Daisy and I were from different planets. She would flip out.

"Okay. The thing is . . . do you remember for a while I was going with this guy, Derek?"

"Sure. Derek Murphy. He's Susan Murphy's older brother."

"Right. But you don't actually *know* him, do you?"

"Well, not the way *you* do, I'm sure." She blew into her cocoa, keeping her eyes carefully away from mine.

"What does that mean?"

She tapped her foot against the stool leg. "Will you please just tell me what you have to tell me?"

I sloshed my tea bag around in the hot water before I continued. "Derek and these two friends of his are sort of mad at me."

"How come?"

"Because I . . . dated them for a while . . . and then we broke up." Why should I tell her the whole story? She was too young to get it anyway.

"You dated these three guys, and then you broke up with all of them?"

"Yeah. Sort of."

"Come off it, Sandpiper."

"What?"

"You twitfungus! How dumb do you think I am? You *dated* them? Everybody knows about you and Derek. And you and Tony Phillips. And you and Chris Shams. And you and God-knows-who-else. It's not a big secret that you give blow jobs to every guy who comes near you."

I spilled my tea down the front of my shirt.

"Did you ever think about what it means for me that my sister does that? Guys talk about you all the time, and not in a nice way. They all wonder if I'm like you. Every time some guy is friendly to me, I have to make sure he knows I don't give head. It's a real conversation starter."

I didn't know Daisy even knew these words.

"You're only in the eighth grade!" I said.

Which made her laugh. "I guess you don't remember what eighth grade was like, do you? Besides, I'm *not* in eighth grade anymore. I'm a rising freshman."

"How long have you . . . known about this?" It made me feel about ten years old to be caught out by Daisy. I could see she was enjoying my discomfort.

"Long enough. Melissa talked to me about it once."

"*Melissa* talked to you? What did she say?"

"Just that she was all worried about you because of the guys you were hanging around with. I told her there was nothing I could do about it—you didn't care what I thought." Her face had turned bright red with either embarrassment or fury, I wasn't sure which. "All my friends know, Sandpiper. It's humiliating!"

What was humiliating was my younger sister lecturing me on humiliation. I scrubbed at the tea stain on my shirt so I wouldn't have to look her in the face. "I'm not doing it anymore."

"Since when? Today? Why would you *ever* do it?"

"Look, Daisy, you're still young. You don't know that much about sex."

"I know plenty. I know it's disgusting to have a reputation like yours when you're barely sixteen."

That made me mad. "You just got your first boyfriend, Daisy, and it doesn't look like he's even hit puberty yet! I don't think you know everything!"

She chugged the rest of her cocoa and banged the cup in the sink. "If this is all you wanted to talk about, I'd rather go shave my legs."

She got all the way into the living room before I called her back. "That's not all. I have to tell you something."

She came back to the doorway and leaned in. "So tell me fast."

"These three guys, Derek and Andrew and Hamilton, they run around together all the time."

"So?"

"So you need to be careful of them."

"*I* do? Why?"

"Because . . . they've made some threats. About you. I don't think they'd really do anything, but . . ."

She took a step closer. "Why would they make threats about me? I don't even know them."

"I guess they're trying to scare me or something. I don't know—they're mad. Anyway, I wanted you to know so you could be careful, and watch out for them. . . ."

Her eyes were blazing holes in my face. "*Watch out for them?* What am I supposed to do if I see them? Am I supposed to spend the summer hiding in the basement? What did they say they'd do to me, if I might ask?"

"It wasn't a specific threat. Derek just said he couldn't wait to see you or something like that. It just sounded weird to me."

She stomped her foot. "*God*, a bunch of sickos are mad at you, so now they're coming after *me*? Why did they think you'd even *care*! Thanks, Sandpiper, thanks a lot!"

"I *do* care! I don't want them to do anything to you. I'm

sorry. I'm really sorry about this, Daisy. Derek sucks."

Daisy gave me a hateful look. "You're the one who sucks. That's how this whole stupid thing got started. You're an idiot and you *suck!*"

She stormed out of the kitchen and went upstairs with the rest of the morally superior women in the family.

Why I Cannot Say What I Mean

Because if I hand you a secret it might look like a wild
animal you should release, or it might remind you of an old
story you'd rather forget. Maybe it won't be as vivid as the
  ones
you're used to. You might leave it out in the rain and let it
  melt.

Or maybe you'll shake the words out of my secret and
  rearrange them
so they make no sense, so no one else will know me as you
  think
you do. Why is the truth always a secret? If I tell you the
  truth,
it would be hot enough to burn us both, and the scars might
  never heal.

I cannot say what I mean because no two people share the
  same
brain. What leaves my hand as love might be tossed into the
  air by you,
or passed along to someone who doesn't recognize it.
What leaves my hand as love might never be handed back.

—*Piper Ragsdale*

Chapter NINE

Colleen has never been too crazy about teaching me to drive. The first time we left the Stop and Shop parking lot, she put on Daisy's bicycle helmet—it was sort of a joke, but sort of not. She tried to be calm, but little whines and stifled shrieks escaped her clenched lips anyway. I think I actually drive better when Nathan takes me out, but I'm not as comfortable. He always wants to have a conversation; he'll be asking me about my thoughts on college at the same time he's telling me to get in the left turn lane. It's confusing. And besides, every time Nathan talks to me that way—*about* something—I remember he's a shrink and this is what he does for a living, and it makes me not want to answer him. So maybe I concentrate more on the driving.

Anyway, I couldn't believe it when Colleen announced one morning that Rags was coming over to give me a lesson. "I don't know when he'll show up, but get dressed when you finish breakfast," she said. "You know how he hates to wait around for people."

"How come *he's* taking me driving?" It was a service he'd

never offered before. And besides, I'd planned to spend the morning writing. Poems seemed to be building up inside me these days, and I loved figuring out how to get them down on the page so they said what I thought I meant.

"Oh, sweetheart, I'm just so busy with last-minute details for the wedding. When your dad called to see if there was anything he could do to help out, I thought this would be good. I know you want to take the test as soon as you can."

"Oh, you *asked* him to." I pulled my robe closed and knotted the belt tightly.

"What's wrong with that?"

"Nothing. I knew he'd never think of it himself."

"Sandpiper—"

"*Piper*," I reminded her.

She sighed. "Whoever you are, don't be so hard on your dad. God knows, he's not perfect. But he's a good guy and he adores you."

"Right."

"Yes, right! What is with you lately?" She shook her head and banged out the front door, on her way to ruin a few more batches of chocolate down at the Sweet Tooth factory.

Even though it wasn't even nine A.M. on a summer morning, my siblingettes were already up and gone. God forbid they should waste a moment of their lovely lives in bed. I slogged upstairs to get dressed.

Usually when I'm around Rags these days, I try to dress in loose-fitting clothes so he isn't tempted to stare at my breasts. There's nothing worse than your own father trying to stop himself from ogling you. But it was hot already and supposed to get hotter. I was tired of wearing sweatshirts for his benefit.

The hell with it. I pulled on a pair of short shorts and a tank top, one that showed my attributes very nicely, thank you.

Rags showed up around ten, the top down on his Mustang. "You're letting me drive *this* car?"

He shrugged. "It's the only car I've got." He threw me his keys, while his eyes traveled quickly over the left one, then the right one, before turning away. When was he going to get used to the way I looked?

"You're wearing that?" he said.

"Yeah." Obviously.

He nodded, keeping his eyes on the horizon behind me and chewing his cheek to pieces. Tough.

"Well, okay," he said finally. "Let's go."

I climbed in behind the wheel, and he got in on the other side. "Dad, would you do me a favor?"

"I thought I already was." He grinned at me, almost like the dad I used to have.

"Would you call me Piper now? I want to start being Piper."

He bobbed his head back in surprise. "Piper? How come?"

"Because Sandpiper is too weird, and Sandy is too normal. I want to be Piper."

He nodded. "Well, I guess if you're old enough to drive, you're old enough to decide on your own name. Piper. I like it."

"You do?"

"Yeah, I do."

Not the reaction I'd gotten from Colleen when I asked her the same thing the night before.

Her eyes teared up, as they did over just about everything these days. Lord.

"But I thought you *loved* the name Sandpiper," Colleen said. "You always make us call you by your full name."

"Only because I hate Sandy even more." I wasn't in the mood to break it to her gently. The constant boo-hooing was getting on my last nerve.

"Oh, that's nice," Daisy said. "Make Mom cry. Just because you decide you have to change your name right *now*, the week before her wedding!"

"This has nothing to do with the wedding! I've never liked my name. Anyway, Piper is *part* of my original name—it's not like I want you to start calling me Gertrude!"

Nathan intervened and explained to everyone, like we were five years old, that it was perfectly natural for a teenager to want a name that seemed to suit her identity better than her birth name did. And he was sure I wasn't saying this to hurt anyone's feelings, blah, blah, blah, and eventually I had to give Colleen a hug and let her smear her wet cheek all over my face in order to get out of the room alive.

Rags's response was a lot simpler. Or maybe he just didn't give a damn.

"Let's get rolling, huh?"

I turned on the car. Fortunately, Colleen's car was a standard shift too, so I was used to clutching and very seldom made that horrible stripping-the-gears noise anymore. I pulled away from the curb smoothly. Really, I was pretty darn good at this now. I think Rags was surprised.

"Hey, you don't even need me. You're an expert!"

"Not quite," I said, but I felt good that I'd impressed him.

"You want to drive to Barlow and see if there are any interesting cases in court today?"

"Really?"

"Sure. Unless you've got something better to do."

"Should I take the highway?"

"You can go the back way if you want."

In the summer, when he wasn't working at the college, Rags was either writing or doing research for his writing. One of his favorite places to get ideas for screenplays was at the superior court in Barlow. I used to go with him sometimes when I was a kid, although we never sat in on anything very juicy. He went by himself to the scuzzy cases. It had been years since I'd gone to a trial with Rags. That, and the whole thing of me driving and him sitting in the passenger seat, made me feel sort of grown up. Like it was *okay* that I wasn't a cute little tomboy anymore, that I was almost sixteen with a body to match.

"Slow it down on the curves a little bit," Rags said. "This car is smaller than your mother's. You're not used to how fast you can go."

"I like this car. It's zippy."

"Yes, it is. But slow it down a little bit. This is a narrow road."

As I came around a curve, I saw someone walking along the roadside. It almost looked like . . . it *was* Walker! God, I hadn't seen him in three days. I guess when you look in a particular direction you have to be very careful not to turn the steering wheel in that direction too.

"Sandpiper! Watch it!" Rags grabbed the wheel and straightened us out. "You were drifting across the lane!"

Walker looked up just as we whizzed past him. I didn't dare take a hand off the wheel to wave.

"Sorry, Dad. I know that guy back there."

Rags looked back at Walker. "Oh."

"And it's Piper, remember?"

He turned around. "Well, *Piper*, you have to concentrate when you're driving—you can't let things distract you. And you were *going too fast*."

"I know. I'm sorry. I'm not used to your car, I guess." I slowed down and drove perfectly the rest of the way into Barlow.

Rags grunted as I parked the car in the lot at the court building. "I don't know why this makes Colleen so nervous. You've got a heavy foot, like most kids, but you know how to drive."

"Well, I didn't when we started," I said, just to remind him that he hadn't been there for the hard part.

Rags went back and opened the trunk. "You know," he said, "it's usually cold in there—the air-conditioning goes full blast. You should probably . . ." He handed me his old navy blue hoodie.

Like I couldn't see through *that* maneuver. What the hell? I put it on, even though I was pretty sure there was no law against bringing big boobs into a courtroom.

Rags checked with the clerk to see what cases were going on. They all know him at the courthouse, so he never has any trouble getting in. But there wasn't much of interest today— a DWI and a couple of larceny cases. We sneaked in quietly to one of the theft trials—Rags likes to watch how people act at dramatic moments—but it was pretty boring. A guy stole a ring from his girlfriend because he said she owed him some money. Both of them chewed gum like they were getting paid for it, so the judge couldn't understand what they were saying, and everything had to be repeated two or three times. I know that's the kind of detail Rags likes, but it doesn't really make for high drama. Still, it was nice to sit there beside him for an hour. God, this was the most time we'd spent together in about a year.

When we came outside again it was hot, and we were both hungry. I unzipped his sweatshirt and threw it in the backseat before getting behind the wheel. Rags would just have to deal with it. He gave me a halfhearted smile and said, "How about stopping at the Dairy King on the way back. I'll spring for burgers and milk shakes."

The Dairy King had always been our favorite place to eat when I was a kid. It was obvious Rags was really putting some effort into this day. If only I didn't know that Colleen had asked him to.

I pulled the car into the DK lot and parked exactly between two other cars so we both had room to open our doors without any possibility of scratching the Mustang's paint.

There was a line of people ahead of us at the window, and within thirty seconds Rags was chatting up the woman ahead of us, joking with her and making her laugh. He has a natural talent. I was looking over the standard menu items (burgers, cheeseburgers, fries, onion rings—all grease, all the time) when somebody walked up next to me and said quietly, "Hey there."

I knew before I looked. Walker. He swirled ice inside a large plastic cup.

"Hi! What are you doing here?"

"I told you. I walk to Barlow sometimes."

"I saw you on the road before. I thought you took the rail trail."

He shrugged of course. "Usually I do. It was buggy in there today, so I came out to the road."

I could feel Dad leaning over my shoulder, waiting to be introduced.

"Um, Dad, this is my friend, Walker. And this is my dad, Rags. Everybody calls him Rags."

Rags stuck out his hand. "Nice to meet you, Walker. I guess you're the reason we almost ran off the road this morning."

"Dad! We did not!"

"I'm kidding. San . . . *Piper* is really a very good driver."

"I'm sure she is," Walker said.

"How do you two know each other? Do you live in Hammond?" Rags asked. I grimaced, knowing how Walker hated to answer personal questions. But he was okay.

"Yeah, I do. Piper and I met in Blessingame Park a few weeks ago."

"Huh! In the park?" Rags said, looking Walker over for signs of depravity. "Well, we're headed back to Hammond. If you can wait for us to get our lunch, we'll give you a ride."

"No!" Walker and I answered together.

Rags looked suspiciously from one of us to the other.

"The thing is, Walker likes to walk," I said.

Walker nodded. "I . . . I don't like cars much."

"You don't like *cars*? Not even a vintage Mustang?" Rags said proudly, pointing to his reliable steed. "You could say no to that?"

Walker looked it over. "It's nice, but no thanks—I'll walk."

It was our turn at the Dairy King window by that time, so Walker gave a little wave and walked off down the road. By the time we got our order, I couldn't see him anymore. I suspected he took the trail back, so we *wouldn't* see him. Meeting Rags had probably freaked him out.

Rags and I carried our billion-calorie lunches to a picnic table. I tried to imagine what Daisy and Rachel would have eaten here. Just the smell of this food could increase your waistline by several inches. I was feeling good though; I was actually starting to think maybe everything was okay, that Rags and I could be buddies again, like old times, until I looked over and saw him glaring at me over his French fries.

"What's wrong?" I said.

"Did you know that boy was going to be here? Is that why you're dressed that way?"

"What?"

"You seem to be wearing as little clothing as possible. I'm wondering if it was for his benefit."

"Dad! You're the one who wanted to drive to Barlow! I didn't know we'd see Walker."

His eyebrows relaxed. "I suppose that's true. Still, the way you're dressed—"

"It's summer! Girls wear shorts and tank tops when it's hot!"

"I know that, but not all girls have . . . look as . . . look like you do." He tried to keep his eyes above my offending female parts, but failed. "And this odd boy you picked up in the park . . . do you know anything about him? He doesn't like *cars*? Who *is* he?"

My milk shake was beginning to taste sour. It was probably

giving me mad cow disease, which Rags apparently already had. Mad dad disease. "God, I didn't *pick him up*. And he's not *odd* either. What's with you?"

"I'm sorry, but he just looked . . . unsavory. Like those boys I saw you with last week."

"Walker is nothing like those other guys. I admit, they're creeps, but he isn't."

Rags was staring at his cheeseburger. "He looked familiar to me. There was something I didn't like about him."

"Will you stop! He's my friend! He's one of the only friends I have left, if you want to know the truth! So just stop saying this crap about him!"

Rags sighed and looked up at the sky, anywhere but at me. "I'm sure you have lots of friends, Piper. You're being overly dramatic. I know it's your age, but when I see you dressed like this . . ." —he waved his hand over my outfit— "I just remember what I was like at your age. You don't understand the way a boy can get excited by something as simple as a low-cut top. Especially *that* kind of boy."

I'd really had it now. "What kind of boy is that? You mean, the kind of boy *you* were?"

His mouth turned down at the corners. He wrapped up his uneaten burger and lobbed it into the trash barrel. "All right. I'm just trying to help you, but I can see you're angry with me. I don't understand *why*, but Colleen told me you were, so I'm not surprised."

Conversation over. Let's not *really* talk about this. I followed him back to the Mustang, only this time he got in on the driver's side. I guess my lesson was over too.

Rags peeled the car in a circle around the parking lot so

that I was thrown against the door before I even had my seat belt on. Damn! I looked over at him. If he was suddenly so interested in my life, maybe I should tell him about it.

"I can get boys excited no matter what I'm wearing. I'm good at it. Do you want to know how I do it?"

The car was stopped, waiting for the traffic to allow us to turn out onto the road. Rags's face was scarlet. I stared at him, but he wouldn't look back.

Finally, as he roared out onto the street, he said, *"No, I do not!"*

Daddy
(with apologies to Sylvia Plath)

You do not do, you do not do,
Anymore, what you used to do.
We were such a pair, we two,
Until my poor white breasts debuted
And grew between us.

Daddy, sometimes it kills me
That I've outgrown you.
I didn't know there'd be no
Follow-through for me and you,
My pa, my pooh.

I have never been scared of you,
But this slow losing of you tears
at my heart and hurts clear through.
I can't even talk to you—you
Who once knew all my secrets.

Funny, you think the glue between us
Loosens as my almost adult self
Begins to act like you. You think
I'm screwing and I'm screwed.
You think I need a talking-to.

Oh, Daddy, Daddy, it's the end
of our duet, the curtain
on our pas de deux.
You're mad; I'm blue.
You're sick of me; me too.

—*Piper Ragsdale*

Chapter **TEN**

When Rags dropped me off after our morning of "lessons," I grabbed a notebook and hid in the window seat to work on an idea I had during our silent drive back to Hammond. There was nobody home but Danny Boy, and he went outside when I came in, so I sat behind the curtain by myself. I was so mad at Rags, I kept punching the pen right through the paper.

Fortunately I was almost finished with the poem when I heard the front door open. By the giggles that followed, I knew Rachel and Daisy were back, but I didn't feel like dealing with the two of them just yet, so I didn't reveal myself.

It sounded like they were unloading stuff on the dining room table, but I couldn't figure out what it was. No doubt they'd gone shopping again and were admiring their purchases.

"You found the best ones," Rachel said. "You've got a better eye than I do." *God, Rachel, you can stop buttering her up now; she worships you already.*

"You found the big scallop shells," Daisy said, "and hauled all those periwinkles up and down the beach."

Oh, gag me. This mutual admiration society was getting old. And why were they out all morning looking for shells? I guess Daisy would do anything to spend time with Rachel. But really, was Rachel planning to schlep a bunch of smelly seashells all the way back to California? They have an ocean there too, don't they?

"What's Piper doing today?" Rachel asked. For some reason, she'd taken to the name change more easily than anybody else. Maybe because she hadn't known me very long as Sandpiper.

"*Piper*," Daisy said, scornfully. "Who knows? Who cares?"

"You two," Rachel said, laughing, "you're so lucky to have each other, and you don't even know it."

"Lucky? I don't think so. If *you* were my sister, that would be luck."

"One more week and I will be."

"Yeah! See me doing the glad-to-have-you-for-a-sister dance!"

How long could they keep this up?

"Daisy," Rachel said, "you know those guys who talked to us on the beach . . ."

"Yeah, they were pretty nice, huh? More proof that Piper the Viper doesn't know what she's talking about."

What?

"I guess I was just thinking about Sam," Rachel said. "I mean, he'd be unhappy if he knew how you were flirting with . . . that one guy."

"He was flirting with me!"

"I know, I know, but don't you think Sam's feelings would be hurt if he knew?"

There was a long silence. Daisy probably couldn't believe her perfect new sister was criticizing her. I was pretty surprised myself.

Finally Daisy said, rather sullenly, "All I did was talk to the guy. I don't think Sam would be mad at me for that. We're not *married*."

"I know," Rachel said. "You're probably right. My mother is always telling me I get *too* committed to my boyfriends. Every time I think, *This is it*, I'm madly in love, and then I'm brokenhearted when it's over, even if I'm the one who broke it off!"

Daisy snorted. She wasn't sure if Rachel was apologizing or not.

"But the thing is," Rachel continued, "you don't really know those guys. They're a lot older than you are—"

"Sandpiper knows them," Daisy said, "and I know Derek's sister."

Derek? They were talking about *Derek?* I flung the curtain back and jumped off the window ledge, yelling.

"You talked to Derek? After what I told you?"

Rachel leaped a foot, and Daisy dropped her sunglasses.

"Lord, Sandpiper! Were you there this whole time?" Daisy picked up her glasses and checked for damage.

"My name is Piper."

"Your name is *Sneak*. Were you *listening* to us?" Daisy demanded.

"Never mind that. I want to know why you were talking to Derek Murphy after I specifically told you not to."

"You didn't say not to talk to him. You just said to be careful of him. But there was nothing to be careful *of*. He was perfectly nice to me."

I glanced at Rachel, wondering how much she'd figured out by now.

"I had a feeling we shouldn't be talking to them," Rachel said. "I remembered them from that day they came up to us on the beach."

Daisy stuck her fists on her hips. "When did you go to the beach with *her*?"

"Were they all three there?" I asked Rachel.

She nodded. "The other two hung back and didn't say much though."

"Yeah, they were kind of dull," Daisy said. "But Derek is really sweet. And cute too." She cocked her head to the side and grinned at me, which I think was supposed to make me feel jealous. She was probably a little shocked that the emotion she'd called forth instead was rage.

"Are you nuts? I told you to stay away from him. He's *dangerous*!"

"He is?" Rachel put her hands on her stomach. "I wish you'd told me that."

"I . . . I guess I should have. I—"

"She was too embarrassed to tell you. She didn't want you to know what a skank she is."

"Shut up, Daisy!"

"You shut up!" she screamed back.

"Stop it! Please!" Rachel had her hands over her ears. "I hate it when you two fight."

We stared at her. Daisy and I were so used to fighting that I don't think it occurred to us it could bother someone that much. Colleen usually just told us to go argue in another room so she didn't have to listen to it.

Rachel took her hands down and sighed, then turned to Daisy. "Why don't you take the shells outside and start hosing them off? I'll come out in a minute, and we'll spread them in the sun to dry."

"Gladly," Daisy said, piling the shells back into the cloth bags. "Anything to get away from *her*." She threw me a nasty look and marched out the back door.

Neither Rachel nor I spoke for a minute or two. Then she said, "You don't need to tell me the whole story. But if Derek is really dangerous, maybe we should do something, tell someone."

"Rachel, honestly, I don't know. But I don't trust him, especially around Daisy. And I can't tell Colleen and Nathan—not now. They've got too much else going on."

Rachel nodded. "Okay. I'm glad I know anyway. I'm with Daisy a lot of the time. I'll make sure she stays away from him."

"Thanks."

"Although—"

"What?"

"Well, Daisy's almost fourteen, Piper. Derek told her how pretty she was. He knew just what to say to her, how to touch her lightly on the arm. He had her eating out of his hand."

My stomach flopped around like a fish out of water. "Shit," I said, leaning back against the wall. "Shit, shit, shit."

Rachel put her hand over mine, the one that was beating a hole in the wall. "It's okay. We'll watch out for her. Nothing will happen to Daisy."

"If it does, it's my fault."

"It won't."

"Tell me if he tries to talk to her again, okay?"

"I will. I'll start telling her how great I think Sam is too. Although what she sees in that goofy little redhead is beyond me."

I smiled. "Lord, you can say that again."

"Don't you dare tell her I said it even once!" She tucked a bra strap back beneath her top and looked out the window. "I better go help her with the shells."

"What are you planning to *do* with them anyway?" I asked.

"We thought it might be nice to spread them out on the tablecloths at the wedding," Rachel explained. "You know, sometimes people put confetti or something on the table between the flower vases, and it just seemed like shells would be more appropriate."

"Won't they be kind of smelly?" I asked.

"Oh, no," Rachel said. "After they're washed and dried, we'll coat them with clear nail polish and then spritz them with a little cologne."

Lord, I was going to be related to Martha Stewart.

Later in the afternoon I was lying on the couch looking at the classified ads as I'd been doing for weeks, hoping that somebody would suddenly need to hire an almost sixteen-year-old to do something other than baby-sitting. After watching the Bradley brats last summer, I had sworn off the nanny thing forever. Nathan said the economy was in a slump, and people weren't hiring. But I couldn't spend the summer hanging out here with Daisy and the newlyweds—I'd go mad.

I heard Mom's car pull into the driveway. Then suddenly she was screaming at somebody, but I couldn't figure out what she was saying.

I jumped up and ran outside, but by the time I got there, she was bent down over something on the lawn. Nobody else was in sight.

"What are you yelling about?"

She turned around with tears in her eyes. "There were boys . . . throwing rocks at Danny Boy. He's hurt!"

Sure enough, Danny was lying on his side in the grass, panting heavily, blood running out of a wound on his head and another on his front leg.

"I saw them!" she said. "They weren't little kids—they were older boys. Why would anybody do this to you, poor old Danny?" The cat squirmed into the shade of her body and let her pet him.

I knew exactly who would do it, but I didn't want to get into the whole explanation now. "Should we take him to the vet?"

"Yes. Run in and get a towel."

Dr. Mankin took us right away, and reassured us that Danny looked okay. He wrapped up his leg and gave us some medicine to make sure he didn't get an infection. "Cats can take a lot—nine lives, you know," he said. "This one's gonna have a headache, but he'll be fine. If he wants to crawl under the bed and hide for a while, just let him do it."

"I feel like crawling under the bed myself," Mom said. "Can you imagine grown boys doing something like this to a defenseless animal? It depresses me to think there could be kids so mean."

Dr. Mankin nodded in agreement.

In the car on the way home I asked Mom if she'd gotten a good look at the guys.

"Well, I saw them, but I was so distraught. One had dark

hair; maybe they all did. One was kind of heavy. I think I'd recognize the tallest one. He had this *awful* look on his face."

Derek. I was thinking I'd have to tell her what was going on, when she suddenly pulled the car to the side of the road. In two seconds she was in full sobbing mode, hands over her eyes.

"I'm sorry . . . you'll have to drive . . . I'm just so . . . this is the last straw." Her weeping got louder as she gave in to it.

"The *last straw*? What else is wrong besides the cat?"

She shook her head. "I don't know. I feel like everything is falling apart."

Oh, Lord. "You mean the wedding? Don't you want to get married anymore?"

She sniffed and tried to stem the waterfall. "Of course I do, but . . . would you get me a tissue from my purse?" She sighed. "Everything is going so fast—I guess I'm just stressed out. Tomorrow is my last day of work at the Sweet Tooth, and I know Nathan thinks I should quit working there after we're married, but I don't want to quit. And Adrienne is so unhappy, and I feel like it's my fault for wanting her in the wedding. And I'm so sick of planning all this stuff, none of which Edie thinks I'm doing right. I feel like the wedding is taking over my whole life, and now this thing with Danny Boy—"

"Slow down, Mom. Danny getting hit with rocks has nothing to do with your getting married."

She sighed and gave me a thin smile. "I know. You're right. It's just that things are piling up, and I'm so . . . scared."

"Scared?"

She shook her head. "I know Nathan loves me, but then I thought Rags loved me too. Once you've been hurt, it's so hard to trust somebody again. I keep having dreams that all these people show up for the wedding and Nathan doesn't. And we can't find him anywhere, and I'm so hurt and embarrassed."

"Yeah, and then I bet Grandma Edie says, 'I told you not to order such a big cake!'"

Laughter burst out of Colleen as if it had just been waiting for its chance. "Oh God, Piper, you're right! She *would*!"

She laughed so hard I had to laugh too. We kept each other going for about five whole minutes. Then I drove home, and Colleen didn't even hold the door handle in her usual death grip.

"I thought you *wanted* me to ask Gil to come out earlier," Nathan said. He and Colleen were supposedly fixing dinner together. If I'd had a chance, I would have warned him that her mood could be measured on the Richter scale.

Colleen was banging pots around. "I said maybe. I didn't say definitely."

"Honey, the wedding is in *five days*. If he's going to come out earlier, it's pretty last minute already."

Colleen sighed. "So he's coming Thursday morning instead of Friday?"

"Yes. I haven't made any appointments after Wednesday, so I'll be able to pick him up and entertain him for the day. All you have to do is get Adrienne to come to dinner Thursday evening."

She groaned. "This is going to backfire, Nathan. She'll see right through it. As soon as she walks in and sees the best man sitting there—"

"Sweetheart, you aren't doing this to hurt her. You want her to be part of your wedding, that's all. Besides, I explained the whole situation to Gil, and he understands completely."

"You *told* him about Adrienne?"

Rachel and Daisy came downstairs, expecting dinner. They smelled like nail polish and cheap cologne.

"Shh." I stopped them. "Wedding argument. Do not disturb."

"Wait till they hear what Rachel and I have been doing! That'll make them happy," Daisy said, ready to march right in and brag about shellacking seashells.

Fortunately Rachel had more sense. "Let's wait a minute, Daisy. They probably want some privacy."

Then we all stood there listening.

"Of course I told him," Nathan said. "You want him to be nice to her, don't you?"

"And wouldn't he be able to be nice to her without being warned ahead of time? Would the mere sight of her make him mean and nasty? Now he'll think she's a nut, on top of being a middle-aged woman with a slight weight problem." Colleen was starting to bubble over.

"Colleen, he's a middle-aged *man* with a slight weight problem. He's been through a bad divorce, his hair is thinning, and he's supporting two children. He's not God's gift either."

"Great. That makes me feel lots better about the whole thing. Adrienne will think we picked him out especially for her."

"You're being silly, honey. They don't have to get married. They just have to get along well enough that Adrienne feels comfortable walking down the aisle with him. I've known Gil since high school. He's a good guy. I promise you he won't make Adrienne feel bad."

"Are you *sure*, Nathan? Because if this goes badly—"

"I am *sure*."

The ensuing silence was punctuated by little wet smacking sounds. Rachel, Daisy, and I looked at each other in horror, and Daisy pretended to stick her finger down her throat. Nothing bonds siblings faster than shared disgust over parental smooching.

Beneath the Bed

The cat has crawled beneath the bed
to hide until his wounds heal.
I wish that tactic worked as well
for me. Hard to believe
pulling a blanket over my head
once made me feel safe.
What a laugh that a drape of bedding
could keep danger at bay.

In those days I kept a box of treasured
objects beneath the bed: a doll too
beautiful to play with, a rain-soaked
disposable camera, my dead grandfather's
hearing aids, and a book of matches
from an Easter brunch at the Apollo Cafe.
Sometimes I'd get the box out to check
my things twice in one day.

My hoarded prizes were my charms
against danger when the greatest risks
were bumblebees, nightmares,
no hand to hold crossing the street.
Now only the cat's beneath my bed.
I understand what *dead* means now,
and unlike the cat,
there's no place I feel safe.

—*Piper Ragsdale*

Chapter ELEVEN

I sat on Calvin Hillenbrand's gravestone for more than an hour and was just about to give up and go home when I saw Walker trudging up the hill, the leather jacket tied around his waist. When I waved at him, he stopped walking for a minute, but then continued on toward me.

"God, I thought you disappeared," I said. "I haven't seen you since that day at the DK in Barlow." I'd walked up to meet him, but he hiked right past me.

"Just been a few days," he muttered. "Bad week." He was talking so low I could barely hear him.

"What's wrong?" I asked, following him. "Have you been sick?"

"Not the way you think."

I had no idea what that meant. He leaned against Calvin's headstone and stared out at the ocean.

"Well, I wanted to tell you that I talked to my sister, like you said I should. I warned her about Derek and his friends. But now I'm afraid it might have backfired . . ." He didn't seem to be paying attention. "You do know what I'm talking about, don't you?"

"What?" He turned to me, but I knew he wasn't really seeing me.

"Walker, I confided this big secret to you, *remember*? About those guys threatening my sister?"

His eyes focused on me. "Oh, sorry. Yeah, sure, I remember. You told her? She knows to stay away from them now?"

"She *knows* to, but she isn't doing it. Derek flirted with her on the beach a few days ago, and now she thinks he's cool or something. Or maybe she just wants to make me crazy—I don't know."

"Maybe the whole thing was a bluff to get you upset."

I shook my head. "I don't think so. A couple of days ago they threw rocks at my cat and hurt him. He's okay, but if my mom hadn't come home when she did, he might not be. It was another threat."

He scowled. "What a sick bunch."

"I told you. They're mad at me, and this is how they're getting even."

"Piper, normal people don't act like this, mad or not. Make sure your sister understands that."

"I'm trying to, but she's my *sister*—she thinks I'm always wrong."

"You have to *make* her understand. Things happen and then it's too late." He kicked angrily at a rock, and it caromed off one headstone and into another.

God, he was gloomy today. I was sure he'd say no to me in this mood, but I promised myself I'd at least ask him. "Listen, the other thing I wanted to talk to you about was this wedding reception thing. You know, after the ceremony's over. I mean, I know you'd never want to sit through *that* part, but I was thinking maybe you could come to the reception, sort of like . . . my date. I mean, not exactly like a date, but just as my friend. It's Saturday afternoon at our house on Jordan Court—number eighteen. There's going to be a band and stuff. Not that you'd have to dance or anything. I know you probably hate stuff like this, but it turns out I'll probably be the only bridesmaid without a date, which doesn't *really* matter to me but . . . you wouldn't have to dress up or anything." *Shut up*, Piper. *Shut up!* God.

Finally his eyes focused and locked onto mine. Ohhh. They were so intense it was hard not to look away.

"Look, Piper—"

"I knew you wouldn't want to. I just thought I'd ask in case you weren't busy—"

"I'm never busy—you know that. But I can't come to your house."

"Why not?"

"Because I'm not good around people. I could tell when I met your dad he didn't like me."

"Walker, it's not that he didn't like *you*—Rags doesn't trust *any* boys because he was such a player himself when he was young. He still is, actually. And he thinks just because I have boobs now, every hormonal male in the vicinity is out to increase his carnal knowledge with me. He's just crazy on the subject of sex, that's all. It wasn't personal."

A smile cracked the corner of his mouth, and he looked away.

"Admit it—I can make you laugh."

He laughed. "You can make me laugh, Piper. But I'm still not coming to that wedding party."

"Oh, come on!" I grabbed his hand without thinking. It was the kind of flirtatious thing I did easily with other boys, but hadn't ever felt comfortable enough to do with Walker. When he pulled away, I knew why I'd never done it before. It was like trying to touch fire.

He got to his feet and faced me. "Piper, listen to me. I don't want you to start getting attached to me. You don't know who I am, and I don't want you to get hurt. I really can't *be* with people. I'm sorry."

"Hey, don't worry about *me*—I can take care of myself. Besides, we've already spent a lot of time together. We get along pretty well, don't you think? I mean, I like to take walks with you and . . . you've been giving me good advice about Derek and—"

"*I can't! You don't understand! I know what you want and I can't do it!*" His long fingers were balled into fists, and he spit the words out at me as if they tasted bad.

I backed up a little. "Okay. I'm sorry. I didn't mean to make you so mad."

"I have to go now," he said, closing his eyes and throwing his head back.

"Just because—"

"Yes. And don't follow me. Okay?" He looked at me again, eye to eye. "*Do not follow me.*"

I felt sick. "I'm really sorry, Walker. I'm sorry!"

But he was halfway down the hill and didn't turn around. I sank back onto Calvin. "What did I do?" I asked him. But Cal didn't seem to know either.

* * *

Back at the ranch, preparations were under way for the big meeting of the best man and the ex-maid of honor. Adrienne was no dope; she'd figured out the scheme as soon as Colleen issued the invitation, but she was coming anyway. Colleen had portrayed Gil as both the nicest man on earth and somebody Adrienne would never be attracted to anyway. "You hate bald," Colleen said. "Nathan says he's almost bald." Adrienne wanted to make sure Colleen knew she wasn't changing her mind about wearing that purple sack down the aisle, no matter who this Gil guy was, and my mother, fingers crossed, assured her she understood.

Gil Steinhart turned out to be a little short, a little shy, a little heavy, but very nice and not at all bald. He was the kind of person who laughed at kids' jokes as if they were really funny, and he didn't feel the need to follow them up with a wisecrack of his own to make sure you knew what a cool guy he was. When I walked in the door, Gil was setting the table, the knives next to the forks, the napkins on the wrong side of the plate. He was wearing a dark blue sweater, which was much too hot for the evening, but it hid his paunch a little bit, which I guess was the reason for the choice.

"Oh, hi there, Piper," he said. "Am I doing this right? I can't remember the last time I set a table."

I rearranged one of the settings, and he followed my lead.

"Thank you. It's a good thing you came in when you did. Your mother would think I was a complete doofus."

"No, she wouldn't. I don't remember seeing either my dad or Nathan ever set a table. In my life, men are usually the ones who bring home the takeout."

He laughed a little. "Nathan is a lucky guy, getting a

wonderful wife and three beautiful daughters too. I envy him." As soon as he said it, he must have realized it made him sound like a pathetic lump, and he immediately changed the subject.

"So, I'm looking forward to meeting your mother's friend, Adrienne. Nathan explained the problem about her backing out of the wedding party, and I said, 'You don't think *I'm* going to be able to fix anything, do you?' But I hope we'll be able to be friends. After all, I won't know anyone else at the wedding!"

I really liked this guy, although I knew if he were sixteen he'd be such a dork I'd roll my eyes every time he walked by. Funny.

"My mother and Adrienne have been best friends for thirty years. Kind of amazing, isn't it?"

"I think it's great. I've known Nathan almost that long, although we haven't lived in the same state for a while now. There's nothing quite like a friend who's known you since you were a dumb kid." He did a double take. "Not that I think kids are dumb!"

Mom and Nathan were making a huge fuss over steaks and asparagus in the kitchen, and Rachel and Daisy hadn't returned from a last-minute grocery run yet, although why it took half an hour to pick up seltzer water and half-and-half, I couldn't imagine. So when Adrienne arrived, it was up to me to make the introductions.

Adrienne had a stiff smile on her face, as though she wanted Gil to know she didn't intend to like him much. I wanted to say, *Come on, Adrienne; he's not a bad guy*, but then I thought she was probably smart enough to figure it out herself eventually.

Nathan came in with a bottle of wine and three glasses, and all the adults but Colleen went into the living room to start getting a buzz on.

Since there obviously was no wineglass for me, I went out to the kitchen to see if I could help Colleen, or at least keep her off the path to insanity.

"Stir those roasted potatoes, would you?" She was leaning against the counter with her own glass of wine, upending it pretty quickly it seemed to me, then refilling it from her own personal bottle. Oh, Lord.

"How's it going out there?" she asked me.

"With Adrienne and Gil, you mean? Okay. Adrienne seems kind of nervous. Actually, so does he."

Colleen sighed. "Oh, what the hell. As long as she *comes* to the wedding. I'm not going to make her walk down the aisle if she doesn't want to. What difference does it make? If she doesn't want to, she doesn't want to. That's that." She took another big swallow.

"She could still change her mind."

Colleen shook her head. "No, you can go first. You'll be my maid of honor. That'll be fine."

"*I'll* be maid of honor? *Me?*"

"Please don't say no, Piper. I couldn't take it. Are you stirring the potatoes?" The kitchen door flew open, and Daisy entered, tears running down her cheeks, followed by a distraught Rachel.

"Mom!" Daisy bent over and pointed to her legs, which had blood running down them from numerous cuts.

"My God, what happened?" Mom finally put the wineglass down on the counter.

"It was an accident," she said, brushing at her tears as Mom got a cloth to clean off her legs and inspect the damage.

"There were these guys," Rachel said, taking over the story. She glanced at me meaningfully, and I knew of course what guys they were. "When we came out of the store, they were sort of flirting with us."

"I know them," Daisy interrupted. "He didn't mean for it to cut me."

"Who?" Mom asked. "What cut you?"

Ignoring the first question, Rachel continued the story. "One of the guys reached in the bag Daisy was holding and pulled out a seltzer bottle. It . . . fell, I guess, and broke, and some of the glass flew up and cut Daisy."

"Why did he take the bottle out of the bag?" Mom wanted to know.

"Just to see what we bought," Daisy said irritably. "I bumped him, and he accidentally dropped it, and it broke. No big deal." She'd sniffed her tears back inside and tried to look stoic.

By the way Rachel was looking at me, I knew Daisy's interpretation was wishful thinking.

Mom was still dabbing at Daisy's legs. "Well, the cuts aren't deep. What a strange thing to have happen."

"We still have one bottle of seltzer though, and the half-and-half," Rachel said, putting them in the fridge. I could tell she was trying to act less disturbed than she felt.

"Why don't I go upstairs with Daisy and put some antiseptic on her cuts?" I offered. "Rachel can stir the potatoes. Mom, you should probably go in and be with Adrienne."

No one objected to my plan. Even though she was upset, I

think Colleen was touched by my wanting to help my little sister. A very touching scene indeed.

As soon as we were upstairs and out of hearing range, I started ranting. "*Now* do you believe me? God, Derek is crazy! I told you he was crazy!"

"I *said* it was an accident. Are you deaf?"

She sat on the toilet lid while I searched the cabinet for ointment, but I was so worked up I kept forgetting what I was looking for.

"Were they all there? All three of them?"

"Yes, but I only spoke to Derek. The other two are scuzzballs." She was carefully patting the biggest cut with a tissue, then examining her own blood as if she'd forgotten what it looked like.

"Daisy, for God's sake, Derek is the biggest sleaze of them all—and the biggest liar. You can't believe him for a second!"

She gave a disgusted sigh. "It's so obvious that you're just jealous because Derek is interested in me now."

"I give up," I said, though I didn't really. I finally located the antiseptic and a tin of bandages stuffed behind three boxes of tampons. Daisy kept jiggling her legs up and down.

"Keep still so I can put this stuff on." Her nervousness told me she was less sure of herself than she wanted me to think.

She was quiet for a minute while I dabbed the white goo on her legs. Those perfectly tanned legs were going to have scars on them for a while. Damn Derek! He'd actually hurt my sister! What was I supposed to do?

"Daisy," I said softly, "can you honestly tell me he didn't drop the bottle on purpose?"

"Can we please change the subject?" She stood up and

walked down the hall to her bedroom. I followed.

"Do you have a long skirt I could wear?" she asked, flipping through the hangers in her closet. "Something with an elastic waist? Pants will be too tight over the cuts."

I had to convince her. "Who do you think threw the rocks at Danny Boy? Do you think that was a coincidence?"

She spun around and stared at me, a glaze of fear finally tinting her eyes. "If you knew who hurt Danny, why didn't you tell Mom?"

"Because she's getting married in two days! I can't dump this crap on her now!"

Daisy stood looking down at the floor for long minutes, more or less paralyzed.

"Come on," I said. "I'll get you a skirt."

As we stood in front of my closet, Daisy whispered, "He likes me. He said so. Why would he want to hurt me?"

"I don't know, Daisy. He's not a normal person."

Quietly, she took the skirt I handed her and put it on. It was too big for her, but it would hide from the company downstairs the ugly cruelty she'd suffered on my behalf.

We needn't have worried about the adults. The wine had loosened them all up, and they were actually laughing. Rachel was putting the savory potatoes on the table, while Nathan stacked steaks in an aromatic heap. We all sat down, the heavily buttered asparagus made its way around the table, and the grown-ups all seemed to be in terrifically good moods.

The four of them kept exchanging giggly little glances until I finally figured it out. Gil liked Adrienne. Adrienne liked Gil. The totally unlikely had come to pass.

It was only the children now who didn't believe in miracles.

Thirteen Ways of Looking at a Black Sheep
(with apologies to Wallace Stevens)

I
Among the happy family
The eye of the black sheep
Is the only black eye.

II
After a while the mind
Of the black sheep
Becomes a black hole.

III
The black sheep turns in a childish
Circle until she makes herself sick.

IV
A man and a woman
Are one.
A man and a woman and a black sheep
Are one too many.

V
One prefers the memory
Of the black sheep,
Her noisy laugh, now gone,
To her actual presence.

VI

The black sheep's icy mood,
Its cause unknown,
Throws a long shadow
Across the window.
Stay inside.
Black ice is dangerous.

VII

Golden sheep will not sit
At the feet of men
As black sheep will.
Or lay their heads
In men's laps.

VIII

Black humor is the invention
Of black sheep.
Without it
People would have to laugh
At themselves.

IX

When a black sheep disappears,
No one notices.

X

Black sheep wear white shirts
So that when they dance
Under the black light
They look beautiful too.

XI

People who live in glass houses
Often mistake
The shadows of birds and
The banging against the window
For black sheep.

XII

The bastard is coming closer.
The black sheep should be moving.

XIII

The wedding lasted all afternoon.
They were dancing
And they were going to dance.
The black sheep sat on her ass
In the driveway.

—Piper Ragsdale

Chapter TWELVE

Adrienne was back on board the wedding train.

She'd stopped by to pick up the discarded purple suit so she could have a seamstress do a few quick tucks in the tummy area (she swore she'd lost five pounds in the past week due to a nervous stomach). There were lavender dresses hanging on doors all over the house so they wouldn't get creased before the big promenade down the aisle. Colleen's wedding dress— off-white silk with a million buttons down the back—was hanging on a hook in the guest bathroom; we were forbidden to so much as brush a tooth in that room. And Nathan, Gil, Rags, Nathan's friend Jack, and Colleen's boss, George, had all just left in the Sweet Tooth van to pick up their rented tuxedos at the mall.

Now that the event was only twenty-four hours away, everybody else was as hyped-up as Colleen had been. Except me, of course. Colleen herself was in the backyard with Edie and the men from the rental company, making sure they put the enormous tent in exactly the right spot between the hydrangeas and the dogwood. (Nathan had assured her he'd be back in time to help with the table arrangements and to talk to the photographer one last time.) Rags had booked the band, and he was supposed to check in with them later on. Rachel, Daisy, and Adrienne were in charge of stopping by the caterer and making sure every single item ordered was going to be delivered, and then visiting the bakery to see how the cake was coming along. (Apparently putting together a three-tiered wedding cake takes more than twenty-four hours.) So as not to stand out as the only unbusy celebrant, I offered to call the florist and double-check on the flowers. That was easy enough.

"Tomorrow? There are no wedding flowers ordered for tomorrow," said the woman who answered the phone. Undoubtedly some flunky who wasn't clued in on all the big events.

"Yes, there are," I said. "Check again. The Rudolph wedding. Eighteen Jordan Court. They're supposed to be delivered before noon."

"Nope. It's not down in my book." She sighed heavily.

"Could I please speak to the manager?" I said. This is what Rags always did when somebody wasn't pleasing him. He called it "going over their heads."

"I *am* the manager, honey. It's not in my book." She pronounced each word as if I were an imbecile.

Shit. How come I had to make this phone call? Why couldn't I be setting up chairs in the yard or watching the pastry chef squirt out pink roses? I tried not to panic. Could you have a wedding without flowers? I suspected Edie would say, no, you couldn't, and I didn't want to be the one to argue with her.

"But I know my mother talked to you about this a long

time ago." Now my voice was edging toward a whine. "The wedding is *tomorrow*!"

The woman sighed again. "Everything is always tomorrow. Look, I'll do what I can. Do you have a list of what she thought she ordered?"

"Yes, I do!" I stared down at the list Colleen had handed me. "Um, a bridal bouquet of Sahara roses and Gypsy Curiosa roses with trailing ivy and amaranth." Whatever that meant. "Four bridesmaid's bouquets with—"

"Hold on. I'm all out of the Gypsy Curiosas. There was a wedding yesterday," she said.

Yeah, well, there's a wedding tomorrow too, I wanted to yell at her, but I remained calm. "Do you have another rose that's similar in color that you could use?"

"Probably," she said.

I took a deep breath. "Okay. And then the four bridesmaid bouquets should be Sahara roses too."

"I think I've got enough of those. You want baby's breath too?"

That sounded repulsive. "Well, the bride wanted lily of the valley in with the roses," I said. The woman grunted. Lord, just let this thing be over already. "Five boutonnieres—"

"Sahara roses with a sprig of green, right?" Like we were so predictable.

"Right. And then twenty-five table vases and two large displays for the wedding couple's table—"

"Twenty-five vases and two big displays? And you want this *overnight*?"

"I told you, my mother ordered it weeks ago."

"And I told you, I don't have it in my book! I'm sorry,

sweetie, but your mother should have checked back before the last minute." Another big sigh. "Look, I'll do what I can. I suppose you want roses in the vases too?"

"The original order was for roses mixed with ranunculus, freesia, Gerbera daisies, anemones, and sweet peas," I said, reading without much hope from Colleen's list. "Would that be possible?"

"No sweet peas, no Gypsies," she said, but her tone had softened. "I'll do the best I can, honey, but at the last minute like this I'm no miracle worker."

"Okay, whatever. But you can deliver to Eighteen Jordan Court before noon tomorrow? It's in the book now?"

"It's in the book. As long as somebody gets a deposit check over to me by five o'clock this afternoon."

"But we already paid you a deposit," I said.

"Sweetheart, if I had the deposit, I'd have your order!"

That was just the beginning. I won't go into the other last-minute hitches, but believe me when I say Colleen was a raving lunatic by the time she coerced Edie into driving a second deposit check down to the florist ("and they're getting a piece of my mind, too"), sent back two hundred brown folding chairs that were supposed to be white, and fielded a phone call from Nathan saying she would have to pick up Gil and him at the tuxedo place because their fancy pants were too short and were being rehemmed, and everyone else had left with George in the Sweet Tooth van.

Adrienne, Rachel, and Daisy arrived home just after Colleen left for Tuxedo Junction.

"Please say everything went okay at the caterer and the bakery," I pleaded.

"Sure," Adrienne said. "You were expecting problems?"

I gave them a quick rundown of the day's disasters and then made up an errand I had to do immediately.

"Don't be long," Adrienne said. "The rehearsal dinner is at seven o'clock and you're not even ready!" God, you'd think I was the one who'd been screwing up everything for the past two weeks. Now that Adrienne had consented to be maid of honor, she seemed to think that made her the leader of the bridesmaid pack.

"Don't worry," I called back.

As soon as I slammed out the door I knew where I'd go. I'd been meaning to walk past the Thai Seasons restaurant for a while now, just to check the area out, but it wasn't on any of my usual routes through town. Of course, I was hoping to run into Walker—I was always hoping that. I told myself I wasn't becoming obsessed with him, but I recognized the signs. Walking past his house like some kind of stalker? How pathetic. I hadn't done that since seventh grade.

But halfway down Jordan Court I heard footsteps behind me and then my name, my old name.

"Sandy?"

I spun around and almost fell off the curb; it was Andrew.

"I just want to talk—"

"Get the hell away from me or I'll scream!" I said, and then I socked him in the arm before he had a chance to move. "I can't believe you attacked my sister! And my cat! An innocent animal—you could have killed him! The three of you are insane!"

"No! That's what I wanted to tell you. Ham and I are out of it now. It's Derek—he's over the edge about this."

"Daisy and Rachel said you were *all* there."

"We *were* there, but it was Derek who smashed the bottle and cut your sister's legs. That was it for us, man. Me and Ham told him to forget it—we thought he just wanted to scare you, not hurt anybody."

I glared at him, trying to decide if he was lying or not.

"Is she okay? Your sister?"

He wasn't getting off that easy. "What about my cat? My mother said there were *several boys* throwing rocks."

"I threw a rock, okay? I'm sorry. I was pissed off at you, Sandy."

"So you try to kill my *cat*? That is the sickest thing—"

"It was Derek's idea! We weren't trying to kill it, anyway. I just wanted to get back at you, that's all."

"For what?"

He shook his head. "You don't even get it. You act like you're crazy about somebody for a couple of days, and then suddenly we're dirt. The way you dumped me, I felt like shit. So when Derek said we were going to get you back, I don't know, it seemed like a good idea."

"Well, it wasn't, okay?" I didn't know what to say to him. It never occurred to me that Andrew might have actually felt bad when I stopped seeing him. I guess I thought guys were only interested in the sex stuff. I figured their balls might hurt, but not their feelings. *Still.*

"I know it was a lousy thing to do—that's why I'm here now. I wanted to say I was sorry and to warn you."

"Warn me?"

"Derek is still mad. I don't know, it seems like he keeps getting *madder*. I think he's going to do something else."

"Like *what*?"

"I don't know, Sandy. I really don't. After the other night Ham and me are staying away from him. He gets really crazy about things."

"You think he'll try to hurt me, don't you?"

Andrew squinted his eyes. "He might. You should be careful, Sandy."

I got a funny taste in my mouth, like I'd been drinking gasoline or something. Like the taste of rotten food or everything gone wrong.

"Yeah, I guess I should," I said. "If I knew how."

I just stood there as Andrew walked back to his car. He gave me a guilty wave as he drove past, but I didn't move a muscle. Should I have thanked him? Apologized for dumping him? Lord, how are you supposed to tell the good guys from the bad guys if nobody is wearing a hat?

I couldn't go back to the house and all that craziness so I finally walked on toward my original destination, although all of the strength seemed to have drained out of my muscles. *Please*, I thought, *let Walker be there. I'll feel safe if I can just see Walker.* Every time a car drove past, I stared at the driver to make sure it wasn't the devil coming to get me. Fortunately, you have to take a lot of back roads to get over to the Thai Seasons, so I didn't feel so conspicuous as I would have walking right through downtown.

When I got there, the restaurant was out of business. Not surprising, I guess. I couldn't remember the last time we'd been there—it was in a rundown part of Hammond, near where a factory building had burned down the year before. The whole area looked pretty abandoned.

Walker had said he lived in an apartment behind Thai Seasons, but there weren't any apartment buildings anywhere that I could see. There was a ramshackle sort of shed back there, with a little porch falling off the side of it and the front steps missing altogether. Surely he didn't mean he lived *there*?

I tiptoed up to a window and looked in, hoping there wouldn't be some stranger staring back at me. At first I thought the place was empty, just waiting to fall down. The walls were missing huge chunks of plaster, and there didn't seem to be any stove or refrigerator in the kitchen. No rugs, no shades on the windows, no signs of life at all. Nobody could live in this place. I moved to another window so I could see more of the main room.

That's when I noticed the mattress in the corner, with sheets on it and a pillow. And next to the mattress stood a pile of books. I flattened my face against the glass so I could see them better. They were library books.

Walker wasn't renting an apartment—he was hiding out in this abandoned shack like a homeless person.

Knowing this secret made me certain there were more I didn't know. If he protected them this well, did I really want to know what they were? Wasn't I in enough trouble already? Did I know Walker any better than I'd known Derek or Andrew? I thought I did, I *wanted* to, but now I wasn't sure.

I hurried back out onto the street, and then, afraid he might come back and see me, I ran.

Secrets

Is it that old coat you wear
that keeps the secrets locked
inside? Wearing a dead man's jacket
is your disguise; the excuse
that it's your dad's only makes the mystery
darker.

I have secrets too,
but I suspect, compared to yours,
mine are merely lies, taboo
tales it wouldn't kill me to tell
someone else besides you. Someone
stronger.

Strange as it seems, I'm the tougher
of us two. If you peeled off that coat,
whatever it concealed would not scare me.
We could go incognito as a couple,
without the secrets, so much
lighter.

—*Piper Ragsdale*

Chapter THIRTEEN

I woke up early Saturday morning, though, God knows, it was not my plan. It was six fifteen and there was a long day ahead, but I just knew I wasn't going to be able to sleep another minute. Already I was wondering if Melissa would show up, if Adrienne would have third thoughts, if the florist would lose her memory again, if Derek would leave me alone for at least one more day. And I knew if *I* was this worried, Colleen must have been up all night.

A glance out the window confirmed it: there she was in the backyard, listlessly deadheading daisies in her bathrobe.

I figured everybody else was still happily conked out, but when I tried the bathroom door it was locked.

"Sorry," came a muffled voice, "I'll be out in a minute."

"That's okay. Is that you, Rachel?"

"Yeah."

"I can wait," I said, but actually I needed to pee pretty badly, so I stood right there by the door. It seemed to me there was some sniffling going on in there.

"Are you okay?" I asked.

The door opened, and Rachel looked at me with red soggy eyes and a quivering chin. "You can come in," she said.

"What's wrong?" I asked, too loudly. She shushed me, pulled me inside, and closed the door again.

"Please don't tell anybody. I'm so embarrassed." She sank down on the edge of the tub and pulled a tissue from a box at her feet.

"I want to know what's going on," I said, jiggling my knees, "but do you mind if I pee while I listen? I really have to go."

She waved at me to go ahead and, gratefully, I did.

"It's stupid, really," Rachel said. "I was afraid this might happen, that I might start freaking out. I mean, all week I've been feeling kind of weird. I thought I could ignore it, but when I woke up this morning and it was the *big day*, I don't know, I just couldn't take it." Tears slid down her cheeks on well-established trails.

I finished what I was doing and washed my hands; then I closed the toilet lid so I could sit comfortably. Rachel kept on weeping as if I wasn't even there.

"Of all the possible people I thought might be freaking out this morning, you weren't one of them," I told her. "You always seem so happy and . . . normal."

"I work on that image," she croaked between sobs.

"Rachel, really, what is going on? Do you want me to get you something? Or wake Nathan up?"

That brought her around. "No! Don't wake my dad. I'd die if he saw me like this. He thinks I'm so perfect." She pulled another wad of tissues from the box and tried to clean herself up. "I'm okay. I just have to *stop* this."

I had no idea what I was supposed to say to her. She was so

completely undone she didn't even seem like the same person I'd been getting to know the past three weeks.

"You must think I'm crazy," she said, trying to smile, but not quite getting there. "The thing is, I feel like I hardly know my father at all. My mother worked hard to keep us apart, and she convinced me it was for the best. But now that I'm around him, I realize he's a really nice person, and I've missed out on him for all these years." The leak began again. "You and Daisy will have more growing-up years with him than I did. Years you'll remember. I mean, I'm happy that he found somebody as nice as your mother to be with, but, on the other hand, I feel so . . . outside . . . like a stranger." She was overtaken by sobs again.

Although comforting people had never been one of my strengths, it would have been inhuman not to move next to her on the tub ledge and put an arm around her. It was funny that she was so upset about missing out on years with her dad—somebody I took for granted already, like part of the furniture. Good furniture. Not to mention that I wasn't having the best relationship with my own father these days, even though he'd never lived more than ten miles away from us and was on good enough terms with my mother to be in her wedding.

"You aren't outside anything," I said. "Nathan wanted you here and you came. Yeah, you missed out on some years, but those would have probably been the yelling years anyway. Now you can know him forever. And you can know us, too. Like Colleen said, there's a bedroom here for you, and you can come whenever you want to."

"Why. . . why. . . ." She took a ragged breath and tried again.

"Why couldn't my mother have been as forgiving as yours? Why did she have to take my father away from me?"

I shook my head. "I don't know, Rachel," I said. It wasn't as embarrassing as I would have expected to have my new stepsister sobbing onto my neck while I put my arms around her. "I don't know why anybody does the things they do. People are weird."

She gave a miserable laugh. "That's for sure."

It occurred to me that I now knew a side of Rachel nobody else around here did. Yes, she was adorable and seemed to have it all together, but *I* knew there was another part of the picture too. Which made me like her all the more.

We sat there so long my butt hurt from the hard porcelain. Finally I made her stand up and wash her face with cold water while I turned on the shower for her.

"You have to get that puffiness to go down before you put on makeup," I said, as if I knew so much about cosmetics.

As I was walking out the door, she said, "Thanks, Piper. I feel better now that I've talked about it."

I shrugged. "Anytime."

She smiled finally. "I'm really glad I get to be part of this family."

"Well, if you're crazy enough to want us, how could we possibly turn you away?"

As I walked back to my room, Colleen was dragging up the stairs. "Are you up already? I thought you girls would sleep longer."

"Daisy's still asleep," I said, "but Rachel and I are up. Just too excited to sleep, I guess."

She sighed. "I'm glad that's how you see it. I'm exhausted.

I want to catch a nap before the hairdresser comes at ten. When Edie shows up tell her . . . tell her . . . oh, I don't know, just keep her away from Adrienne."

"Yoo-hoo!" came the familiar greeting from downstairs. "I hope you're all up and ready for breakfast! I brought bagels and lox. There's lots to do!"

Colleen's eyes expanded. "And keep her away from me, too!" she whispered. "Please! For two hours!" She scuttled down the hall and sneaked into her room, leaving me to deal with my grandmother on my own.

By noon we were in full swing. The hairdresser had made the rounds—Colleen, me, Daisy, Rachel—and was finishing up on Adrienne, who was annoying the hell out of someone who'd already dealt with four other fussy females that morning.

At two minutes past twelve I started worrying about the florist. What if they forgot us again? But ten minutes later the van pulled up, and two men began carting large vases into the backyard. The tables already had white tablecloths on them, held down at the corners by clips because the day was pleasantly breezy. The weather forecaster had said there was no chance of rain—it would be the perfect Saturday for swimming, boating, and other outdoor recreation, like getting married.

Daisy and Rachel (whose face was now pink and shining) had already spread their polished shells in the center of the tables, leaving room for the flowers, of course, and I had to admit the effect was pretty. The band members were setting up a small platform at one edge of the tent so they'd be ready to play the hokey processional for the ceremony before launching into something more lively at the reception. At the far end of the garden there were two hundred white chairs set up with a path through the middle that led to the rose arbor under which the actual deed would be done. The photographer would be here at one o'clock, and we'd all be dressed and ready to pose for a ridiculous number of unnatural shots that we'd complain about later. Daisy and I had neither heard from nor spoken of Derek for more than twenty-four hours. Basically all was well.

Until Daisy came running out of the house in a bathrobe and bunny slippers. "Piper, where's Grandma Edie's corsage? They brought the bouquets and boutonnieres into the house, but there's no corsage!"

Crap and double crap. "It wasn't on the list! Colleen gave me a list, and there was no corsage for Edie on it! How was I supposed to know?"

"You mean you didn't order one? There *isn't* a corsage for her?" Daisy's eyes got huge.

"This is my first wedding, Daisy. There wasn't even a bouquet for the bride when I called this place. I wasn't thinking about a corsage for Edie."

Daisy looked desperate. "We'll have to make one then. If she finds out we didn't order her one, she'll have a fit."

"Make one? How are we supposed to do that?"

Daisy looked around at the vases and displays on the tables. "I can make one. Go into the laundry room where Mom stored all her craft stuff when we moved here. She has some thin wire in there from when she made those wreaths that time. Get me that and a scissors and some lavender ribbon."

"Where's the ribbon?" I was so happy Daisy had an actual

plan I would have done anything she said.

"Should be in there too. In a white box that says 'Ribbons.'"

"We have a box that says 'Ribbons'?"

"Hurry up! And don't let anybody see you! Especially Edie."

By the time I found all the supplies requested, Daisy had plucked a small arrangement of two roses, freesia, and greens from the outdoor displays. Carefully, she wrapped the wire around the cut stems, then wrapped the wire with ribbon, and finally tied the whole thing with a tiny bow.

"How did you learn to do that?" I asked her.

"I know what a corsage looks like. It's not that hard."

"God, you did a good job. I don't think she'll know."

"That's the whole point, Piper!" I looked at Daisy to see if it was obvious that aliens had taken over her body, or if she had miraculously grown up overnight.

Edie loved the corsage, which we said had gotten mislaid with the outdoor arrangements. The creamy roses looked lovely with her sage green dress, and she was, at least momentarily, pleased.

As we lined up on the porch in ascending order according to size and shades of purple, it all suddenly seemed very serious and *important*. Which I guess it sort of was.

The musicians were waiting for the last-minute guests to find seats before starting the processional. The last people to rush in were the Renfrows, Melissa following her parents to back-row chairs. I wondered if they were late because Melissa had had to be coerced into coming.

I noticed Laura King was seated in an inconspicuous back row too. I knew it must be her because, right after she sat down, Rags went over and gave her a kiss. Not a big smooch or anything, just a cheek kiss, but it shocked me anyway. Even though I knew he had girlfriends, I'd never actually *seen* him with another woman. Why did everybody have to reveal their big secrets at the same time?

The longer we stood there, the odder the whole thing became. Standing up under the rose arbor, waiting, was Nathan, a goofy smile raising his cheekbones up to his ears. Next to him was Gil, and then Rags, also smiling, although a bit sheepishly I thought—probably because his ex-mother-in-law was sitting in the front row cursing him under her breath. And how strange was it that two hundred people were sitting on folding chairs in the backyard waiting for Colleen to appear as though she were royalty? It was all ridiculously weird, and ridiculous too that it made me want to cry.

Fortunately the music started up, and we marched in as planned, took our places to the side of the arbor, and watched the usual ceremony take place, which only seemed bizarre, I'm sure, because it was my mother in the wedding dress. The vows, the rings, the kiss, nothing out of the ordinary, except it was Colleen, suddenly not at all tired, but quite beautiful in her silky creamy dress, being married to a nice man who was not my father.

It was over in twenty minutes. When the music began again, we marched back down the aisle while two hundred people stood up and watched. I walked with Rags who put my hand on his arm and held it there as if we were at the debutante ball. We walked across the yard and formed the receiving line the way that Edie had ordered us to, with Colleen and Nathan at the beginning and the rest of us lined up next to them. The line ended at the tent where people could finally get out of the sun and get something to drink.

I stood in line between Rags and Colleen's boss George, both of whom knew everybody and were way too gabby. I saw that my job would have to be keeping the guests moving along if the real party was going to get started. At some point I realized Edie was standing in back of me, down a little way, loudly introducing Rachel to everyone walking by. Of course. Edie realized Rachel didn't know *any* of these people, and she was trying to be helpful. Or maybe she was just trying to be socially correct, but whatever the reason, she was right this time.

I looked across George to see how Rachel was doing. Her bright smile was starting to sag at the corners—that couldn't be good. She glanced at me with a look of panic in her watery eyes. I did the only thing I could think of.

"Rachel," I said, "why don't you come down here and stand by your dad?" Without waiting to hear whether Edie approved of this break with tradition, I took Rachel's hand and pulled her past George, then maneuvered her in front of Rags, Adrienne, and Gil so she was in her rightful place, next to the only person she really wanted to be with today.

Nathan immediately put his arm around her, as I knew he would. He bent to kiss the top of her head and then began to introduce her to people as his daughter. Rachel leaned into his side a little, but lost the look of imminent meltdown she'd had when she was stuck at the end of the line with Edie. I was almost jealous of her, the way she adored Nathan and he adored her right back. Here I was standing next to Rags and feeling like I'd rather step on his toes with my high heels than have his arm wrapped around my shoulders.

There was an awkward moment or two when the Renfrows came through the line. Mrs. Renfrow gushed over every-thing—my dress, my hair, my bouquet—she couldn't stop complimenting me. Mr. Renfrow nodded and smiled, but he seemed a little flustered too, as if I wasn't the same girl who'd hung out at their house for years. Melissa had probably told them some story about me. Not the whole story though, not the part where she said to Allie and me, "Don't be dorks. It's no biggie. Everybody does it if they're cool." I'm sure the Renfrows were shocked; I *wasn't* the same girl anymore as far as they were concerned.

Melissa seemed calm compared to her parents. "I didn't realize your stepdad had a daughter," she said, looking at Rachel. "Now you have two sisters."

Melissa, an only child, had always longed for a sister, even though I told her how awful they could be. She was blind to Daisy's faults, though I'd eagerly pointed them out for years. But now I sort of understood it. There she was, sandwiched between her mother and father, the only kid getting squashed in the middle of all that parenthood.

I smiled at her. "I kind of like the new one. But you can still have Daisy if you want."

"It's a deal," she said, just as Daisy spied her and leaped out of line to give her a hug. I guess she'd been missing her too.

Finally all the hands had been shaken (although I noticed Laura King detoured around the receiving line), and we were allowed to join the party under the tent. The band was play-ing, and the caterer was putting out plates of appetizers. I was headed toward the long table where the wedding party was supposed to sit, so I could slip off my awful purple heels, which were killing me, when I saw him standing just inside the gate, hands jammed in his pockets, looking ready to bolt.

"Walker! You came!" I said as I limped down the path. "I thought . . . you said you wouldn't."

He shrugged, of course. "I don't know. I haven't seen you in a few days, and I felt bad about getting mad at you. It wasn't your fault."

"That's okay. I'm glad you're here."

"Am I dressed all right?" He brushed at his pants leg.

"Sure," I said, although people were noticing him as we walked into the backyard—his sneakers, khaki pants, and short-sleeved shirt stood out a bit from the general finery on display. Still, I could tell he'd made an effort to look good; his hair was even combed. And, Lord, he wasn't wearing the jacket!

When he saw the tent full of milling bodies, he backed away. "There are so many people here. I shouldn't have come."

"Yes, you should have!" I grabbed his hand, which took all the courage that the lavender dress afforded me. God, holding hands was a big deal now? Who was I anyway?

We didn't see Rags come up in back of us. "Walker, isn't it?" he said, sticking out his big paw. He was looking at Walker out of the side of his eyes, a very suspicious look. "What did you say your last name was again?"

The Ache of Marriage
(with apologies to Denise Levertov)

Two by two
we walk the aisle
away from the rose arbor,
my mother and her husband,
my father and me.

My mother's husband
is someone else's father.
She wears a dress similar
to mine but stands farther
from the bride.

A perfect day, the guests say,
referring to the sun, the
flowers, a cake as tall as
a woman, seated,
with roses in her hair.

Guests do not see
the ache of marriage,
or perhaps they look away.
This is the day that make-
believe feels real.

The other girl in the other
new lavender dress
knows what I know.
We are the ache of marriage,
the truth ache.

—*Piper Ragsdale*

Chapter FOURTEEN

"My last name?" Walker repeated.

"Yes, I don't think Piper mentioned it when we met at the Dairy King." Rags's smile looked evil. I wanted to kick him in the shin, but instead I said the first thing that came to my mind.

"Percy! His name is Walker Percy." The name had leaped into my mind with a familiar ring. Even as I said it I was hoping it wasn't somebody we knew.

"Really?" Rags said. "Walker Percy? Did you know there was a well-known Southern writer by that name? I've always admired his work."

Damn. That was where the name came from—I'd seen the books on Rags's shelf. But once I start lying, I usually keep going. There's always a chance you can get away with it.

"That's who he's named for. His mother loved that author too." Walker was staring at me like I was bonkers. He was so nervous he couldn't stand still.

But Rags wasn't finished with the inquisition. "Is your family from around here?"

"Um . . . ," Walker stuttered, "sort of. I mean, not right here in Hammond, but . . . nearby."

Rags narrowed his eyes. "Why do you look so familiar to me?"

What was up with Rags anyway? Walker just stared at him, totally freaked out, so I answered for him. "Don't know, Dad. We want to get something to eat now." I tightened my grip on Walker's hand, even though he was barely returning the favor, and moved him out of the hypnotic glare of Rags's headlights. I don't think he would have been able to move otherwise.

But by the time we got to a table, Walker was looking back nervously. "I have to go. I really have to. Your father . . . he doesn't like me."

"Oh, who cares? I don't like his girlfriend either."

Walker stared at me.

"Not that you're my boyfriend. I didn't mean that."

But he was only worried about Rags. "You don't under-stand. I really have to go."

"Just because my father is being a jerk? He doesn't know you. How could he?"

Walker looked down at his shoes. "I don't know."

"Stay for a while. You came all the way over here."

His gaze traveled slowly up from the ground, brushed my dress, skimmed lightly over my breasts—which made me inhale sharply—and rested on my face. "You look pretty. You look very pretty."

Before I could breathe again, he was gone—down the path and through the gate—disappeared.

I didn't go after him. For one thing, my shoes hurt, and I knew he'd be two streets away before I could limp to the front sidewalk. But I think I also didn't want to talk to him just then. I didn't want him to say anything that might break the spell of what he'd already said. I was trying to remember if anyone had ever told me I looked pretty before. Oh, yeah, Colleen probably had. But no boy my age. They might say I looked hot or sexy, but not pretty. Rags might have said it when I was a kid, before he started thinking I looked like a slut.

I slipped my shoes off and stuck them under a bush—the grass felt good under my hot feet.

"Wasn't that that guy who walks all over town? Do you know him?" Melissa had come up behind me holding two glasses of punch. She handed one to me.

"Yeah, that's him."

"So, are you . . . ?" She grimaced and let me figure out the end of her sentence myself.

"*No.* God, I don't do it with *everybody.* He's my *friend.*" It was true. Walker was probably the first male friend I'd ever had, and I didn't want to wreck whatever was between us just for some sexual power trip. I definitely wanted our friendship to go somewhere, but I was willing to wait to see just where that might be.

"Sorry, I just thought—"

I lowered my voice. "I'm trying not to do it anymore, Melissa."

Her mouth screwed up into a half-smile. "You have to *try* to stop? It's like an addiction or something?"

I guess she meant that as a joke, but it seemed to me she was right. "Maybe I'm addicted to the way guys treat me when I'm doing it. How much they, sort of, love me."

Melissa took a step backward. "You think they *love* you?"

I shook my head. "I know they don't really, but just for those few minutes, it *feels* like they do."

Melissa was quiet for a minute, like she was thinking about it. "So, what's his name?" she asked finally. "The walker guy."

"I don't know. I just call him Walker, and he calls me Piper. It's fine that way."

"He won't tell you his *name*?" She shook her head, not able to understand me anymore, not willing to try.

But it was okay. We got plates of appetizers and sat on the porch swing for a while and talked about neutral subjects: teachers, driving, her job at her dad's office. Nothing important. And when her parents said they had to leave, even though the main dinner was just being served and the band was revving up, she didn't ask them if she could stay, and I didn't ask her to either.

It wasn't a bad party. I even danced with a couple of people. Of course, there weren't any guys my age there, except for Rachel's beach boy, Mark, and he was busy keeping her mind off the trauma of her father's wedding. George danced with me, and so did Gil Steinhart, although he and Adrienne were practically inseparable most of the afternoon, laughing and talking at a corner table. I had to dance with Rags, of course— one of those wedding traditions or something—but he held me stiffly, like I was some ancient old lady he was afraid he might break. Neither of us said a word. I was mad at him anyway for chasing Walker away, and for bringing a date to Colleen's wedding, and for treating me like an acquaintance instead of a daughter. When Nathan danced with Rachel, she was crushed to his chest.

Daisy's boyfriend Sam was there too, but they didn't dance. It wasn't music kids know how to dance to, and anyway, they were still a little shy with each other, the way you are at that age. Thank God! I was so glad to see her acting like the kid I knew again. I started thinking about the first time I went to the movies with Tony Phillips and could barely speak to him. How had my life changed so fast? Could you stop the changes? Could you go back?

By seven o'clock I was so tired I could barely move. I'd eaten too much shrimp and too much wedding cake, and I just wanted all these people to go home so I could go to bed. Nathan and Colleen had finally gone inside to change into their traveling clothes—their flight to Hawaii left at nine, and George was driving them to the airport in the Sweet Tooth van, which had been decorated with streamers and tin cans for the occasion. You wouldn't think adults would do this stuff.

The newlyweds came out of the house to more shouts and applause. Lord, hadn't we worshipped them enough today? They wanted to talk to Rachel, Daisy and me before they left. Rags joined us, uninvited.

"I know you girls are all old enough and smart enough to take care of yourselves for ten days," Nathan said. "But now I sort of wish we were taking you with us." He looked longingly at his daughter, and Rachel teared up again.

"Since Rachel is the oldest, she's in charge," Colleen said. "And if you need us for *anything*, the number is next to the phone. You can call day or night."

"Or you can call me," Rags said. "I'm not that far away. No sense bothering these guys on their honeymoon for something small."

"Can we call you day or night?" I asked. "I mean, will you be at home? Or should we have another number for nights?"

Rags's face reddened. "You can always leave a message, Piper. That's what answering machines are for."

Colleen interrupted. "I'm just saying, don't be afraid to call us if you need to. We'll call you to check in every few days too." She looked a little teary herself. "Gosh, I've never gone anywhere without you two in my life!"

Daisy gave her a hug. "We'll be fine, Mom. Don't worry. Have a great time!"

I obviously had to do and say the same.

But Rachel was breaking under the strain of the long day. "Dad, Daddy . . ." she started, but then the tears began to pour. "I'm so glad I was here," she choked out. "I'm so glad—"

"Me too, baby. Me too." Nathan clutched her to him and let her cry for a minute, but she was embarrassed to have so many people witnessing her sogginess, so she transferred her body to Mark as soon as she could. He seemed more than willing to receive it.

Then there was the ritual throwing of the birdseed, and the climbing into the candy truck, and off they went. Once they were gone, people began to drift away pretty quickly. The band played for another hour, but the caterer started cleaning things up. It was over at last.

Except not quite. I was collapsed on the porch swing when Rags appeared, a grim look on his face. He sat in a wicker chair and stared at the top of my head.

"What?" I said.

For a change he allowed his eyes to meet mine. "I know who that boy is. I remember now."

"What boy?" I knew immediately who he meant, but I didn't want to. The look on his face promised bad news.

"Walker. *Walker Percy*. That's a good one. At least he's literate." Rags shook his head.

"He didn't tell me his name was Walker Percy. I made that up. He didn't lie to me."

"I bet he hasn't told you the truth though, has he? Do you know what his real name is?"

I chewed my lip and picked at my lavender hem.

"No, I'm sure he didn't. His name is Aidan Blankenship."

Aidan Blankenship. A nice name. "So? Is that supposed to mean something to me? Is Aidan Blankenship a murderer or something?"

Rags sighed. "Not exactly."

I stared at him. "What are you talking about? How would you even know anything about him?" I stood up and headed for the house. "He's my friend, and I don't feel like listening to some dumb lie."

"It's not a lie, Piper. Come back here and sit down. If he's your friend, you should know this about him."

I didn't sit, but I walked back so I could see Rags's face.

"I finally remembered where I'd seen him before," he said. "At the court in Barlow about a year and a half ago."

"Are you sure it was him? You see so many people in court . . ."

He looked me right in the eyes, almost as if I didn't have boobs. "I'm sure. It was a case I couldn't get out of my mind for a long time. I think you should sit."

I eased myself back onto the swing reluctantly. This could not be good, and I didn't want to hear it.

"Aidan was on trial for manslaughter. It was his older sister who pushed for the trial—she was kind of crazy, I thought. The jury was sympathetic to Aidan and let him off. The sister was looking for some way to hurt him, I think, to get back at him."

"Why? What did he—"

"Aidan ran over her three-year-old son with his car and killed him. He killed his nephew."

My mind was circling around the words, not grabbing onto them.

"That can't be right. Walker, or Aidan, won't even *ride* in a car!"

Rags nodded. "Well, that makes more sense now, doesn't it? He didn't hit the boy on purpose. As I remember it, he was backing out of the driveway and just didn't look. He'd had his license only a short time. He didn't see the boy. It was one of those tragic stories. His family just couldn't seem to forgive him."

Oh, my God. Poor Walker! Suddenly everything I knew about him started to make sense. Walking everywhere, checking tire marks on the street, having no family to live with.

"If it was an accident, why didn't they forgive him?" I rose to my feet again. "They just threw him out? His sister wanted him to go to jail?"

"I don't know all the details, Piper. I was just there for the trial—I don't know what happened afterward, but it does seem like he's on his own now. And obviously he's kind of a strange guy. Solitary, walking around all the time. Going through something like that does a job on your head. I'm telling you this because I don't think you should expect to have a normal *friendship*, or whatever you call it, with this person."

I glared at him. "Do you mean that I should abandon him too? Like everybody else has? That's a great idea."

"I'm not saying that. I'm saying you shouldn't expect much of him. He's . . . he's damaged."

Damaged. What a horrible word. Like a car after a wreck. A house after a fire. The seashore after a hurricane. It was how I'd been feeling myself. Slightly ruined, a big mess.

Rags reached out for my hand. "I know you like him. I can tell. I just don't want you to get hurt."

I ignored the hand and brushed past Rags into the house. "Too late for that," I said. "Way too late."

Damage and Sorrow
for Aidan Blankenship

There is no warning. The tornado hits, the fire
engulfs, the day turns black and blacker.
You fall and you keep on falling, but there is no
bottom on which to rest.

The rest of the world goes on without you.
You are not in their line of vision—up a tree
maybe, or on your knees, you cannot
find a pair of eyes to meet.

I will meet you at the crossroads of damage
and sorrow. We will recognize each other
by the ragged holes in our hearts, sorry
for everything, hoping to come home.

Let me walk you home. To the shack,
to the beach, to the trail in the woods—
I'm looking for a way inside. When I find it,
I'm warning you, I will not leave.

—*Piper Ragsdale*

Chapter FIFTEEN

Daisy had been too hyperactive to stay home with just us after a day coated in romance and buttercream frosting, so Rachel told her she could spend the night at her friend Stephanie's house. I suspected Sam would be showing up there too, which probably also crossed Rachel's mind, but I think she needed to collapse into bed and not listen to anymore of Daisy's chatter. Besides, Stephanie's parents were probably better equipped to keep amorous eighth graders apart than we were. With everyone gone, the house was suddenly quiet. Of course, I wasn't going to be able to sleep anyway. I took off my dress and crawled under the bedspread in my underwear—locating a nightgown was too much work.

My head was spinning with the news of the day: my feelings about the wedding, my feelings about my father, my feelings about Walker (or Aidan, if that's who he really was). They were all jumbled together in a big knot of emotion I couldn't untie. Finally I had to sit up and write a few poems, just to get some of the feelings out where I could see them. Writing poetry was becoming a serious addiction this summer. I decided, since

Ms. Eldred was a poet, I should probably sign up for her honors English class in the fall.

The writing helped a little, but I was still wide awake hours later when I heard a loud noise, or almost *felt* it, like a crash or a gunshot, I thought, very near our house. I pulled the bedspread up over my head like a kid would, and squinted my eyes closed so as not to see whatever was going on, but nothing else happened—no second shot, no screams, no police sirens. The longer I lay there, my heart thumping against my ribs, the more I wondered if I'd made it up. But that was impossible—I'd heard *something*.

Finally I got up and walked to the door of Rachel's room. No sound—she must have passed out after all that crying. I went back to my room for slippers and a robe, and then turned on the light in the hallway. I had no intention of going outside to investigate, but I thought maybe I'd be able to see something from the living room window. As soon as I turned on the light, Danny Boy scooted up the stairs and into my bedroom, faster than I'd seen him move since he got hurt. He was spooked, which meant he'd heard it too.

But there was no noise now—everything had returned to middle-of-the-night quiet. The light from the hall was enough to dimly illuminate the downstairs. As soon as I turned the corner into the living room, I saw what had happened, but it took me a minute of standing and gawking to put it all together.

The window over the couch was broken, glass had sprayed across the room, the curtain was blowing in the breeze, and a rock the size of a baseball was lying on Nathan's Oriental carpet. It hadn't been a crash or a gunshot—just the window being demolished by . . . who else?

Avoiding the debris as much as possible, I walked across the room and picked up the rock. There was a rubber band around it, and under the rubber band, a note, scribbled in black marker:

It's your turn now, Sandy. See you soon!

Christ, Derek was demented! I pulled the note off and put the rock back on the rug where it had been; then I ran up the stairs to my room, locking the door behind me. For the next two hours, until the sky began to get light, I sat at my desk listening for any suspicious rustle or creak in the house, obsessively reading over the eight-word message, then jotting down my own words, not exactly a poem, but something to help me make sense of all this rage that was being directed at me, something to keep me sane until I dared to unlock the door.

By 5:30 it was light enough. I got dressed and wrote my own note, for Rachel, and taped it to her door:

Rock broke the living room window—don't worry— I'll be back soon.—Piper.

I knew she'd put two and two together, but I figured I'd be back to remove the note before she woke up. It was chilly outside, or maybe I was just cold; I put on a sweatshirt and stuck Derek's note in a pocket. It occurred to me to call the police, but I knew the first thing they'd do was call Rags. I couldn't imagine dealing with him right now. There was only one place I could think of to go.

I ran all the way across town to the shack, looking over my shoulder the whole way. By the time I got there, I was totally out of breath and scared shitless. I banged on the crooked front door—there was nobody else around here anyway except the one person I needed to wake up.

"Walker!" I yelled. "Let me in! I know you're in there!"

The door was jerked open more quickly than I'd expected. I hadn't woken him up—he had on his leather jacket, as usual, and looked ready to go out.

"What are you doing here?" he asked, in a very unwelcoming voice.

"I didn't know where else to go," I said. "Can I come in?"

His eyes locked on mine as though searching for clues.

"Please let me in!" I begged.

He stood back then and opened the door so I could enter, sweeping his arm low, like a butler at a mansion. "How did you know I lived here? Did your dad figure that out too?"

"What? No, you told me you lived behind the Thai restaurant, remember?"

He grimaced. "But your father . . . he knows, doesn't he? I could tell the way he looked at me. I guess he told you the whole story."

I hadn't been thinking about yesterday's drama, but my memory kicked in. I nodded. "He told me."

"*How* did he know?" he asked, his teeth clenched. "I thought I was being so careful."

"He's a playwright. He goes to the court in Barlow to listen to cases. He remembered you."

"I bet he did." His normally kind face crinkled into a scowl. "So how come you came here? If you think I need somebody to talk to, you're wrong. I don't talk about it, ever, to anybody. And I never will." He picked a bowl off the floor, and a small towel, and shoved them into the top of a half-filled garbage bag.

"That's not why I . . . What are you doing? Are you running away or something?"

"Running away?" He laughed a miserable laugh and hoisted the bag to his shoulder. "Walking away is more like it. There's nothing to run from anymore, but there's always a reason to leave."

"What's the reason this time? Because I know who you are? Because I know about the accident?"

His face turned gray. He flung the garbage bag at me, and it knocked me off balance so I banged into the wall. *"Don't talk about it!* You don't *know* about it! You *don't know anything!"* he screamed at me as he made for the door.

"Wait! Please! I'm sorry! Don't leave!" I yelled after him. "I need your help, Walker!"

He'd already jumped down from the saggy porch, but he stopped and looked back. "I can't think of any reason why anyone could possibly need *my* help." His eyes were as dark and deep as a dry well.

"I don't know who else to go to," I said, as I took the note from my pocket and handed it to him. "This was wrapped around the rock that was thrown through my living room window a few hours ago."

He read it quickly and looked up at me, his face now one I recognized. "From that same crazy guy?"

I nodded. "Derek. And my mother and stepfather just left for their honeymoon, so it's just the three of us home alone. I'm worried. I thought at first he was just bluffing, but now I think he's really nuts."

"No doubt about it."

"What should I do?"

He handed the note back to me. "Call your father," he said flatly. "He'll help you."

"No! I can't call him. I won't ask him for anything."

"Then you'll have to call the police, I guess." He was making it very clear that this was not *his* problem.

"And then *they'll* call my father. I don't want him involved in this!"

Walker sighed. "Look, Piper, I wish I could help you, but I can't. Especially now. I have to get out of here."

"Why? Are you leaving just because my father knows your name is Aidan Blankenship?"

He flinched when I said it. "Don't you get it? I don't want to *be* Aidan Blankenship. I like being the Walker—no name, no address, no phone, no friends. That's who I am now." He tried to turn aside, but I stepped in front of him. I understood what no friends meant, and I was not letting him get away with that.

"We're not friends? What are we then?"

He looked away from me, toward an old vacant factory building. "It was a mistake. I shouldn't have let you think we were friends."

I gave his shoulder a rough shove. "You didn't *let* me think anything. I'm not an idiot. We *are* friends, whether you like it or not."

He glanced at me quickly, then away again. "Whatever. I can't explain this to you, Piper. I just have to go." He ducked back inside the shack long enough to pick up the garbage bag and then jumped down off the porch and started walking.

And so did I. "I can walk as long and as far as you can," I said.

He shrugged and kept on walking, taking long strides. I stayed with him, making my own legs stretch as far as they

could. It felt good to walk, to pretend I was going somewhere that I was not locked in my bedroom, worrying about that moron Derek. I would go wherever Aidan Blankenship went

After two blocks he stopped suddenly and threw down the bag. "What are you doing, Piper? You can't come with me. I don't even know where I'm going."

"Neither do I. I guess we'll see when we get there."

"You can't come! What about your sisters? They'll be worried!"

That was true. I wondered if Rachel had woken up yet and found my note and the broken window. Surely Derek wouldn't come back to the house in broad daylight, would he? Rachel would probably call Rags when she figured out what had happened. Another reason I might as well keep on walking with Aidan.

"I'll call them later," I said. "I'll tell them I'm hiding from Derek."

Aidan groaned. "Why are you so crazy?"

I shrugged. "I don't know. Why are you?"

After a few seconds the little half-smile struggled to appear. "I give up."

"Good! I'm starving! Let's get breakfast at the Bluebell Diner—it's just a few blocks from here."

He shook his head as if he didn't know what to make of me, but he let me take his hand carefully in mine. We walked to the Bluebell like that, linked.

My Turn Now

Is it my fault
you're angry enough
to break things?
I gave you the kind of love
I thought you wanted.
I thought I wanted
to give you the kind of love
you let me give.
Did you think that meant
you owned me?
I don't owe you any more
than I want to give you.
Is it my fault
because I left you,
or would you hate me
by now anyway?
You're angry enough
to break things,
but it's not my fault.
You can hurt me,
but I don't think
you can break me.

—*Piper Ragsdale*

Chapter SIXTEEN

"Are you sure your father would freak if you told him?"

"He'd go apeshit. He thinks having breasts and wearing a tank top are mortal sins, at least for me. Although I think it's a prerequisite for his girlfriends." We were in the corner booth at the Bluebell, and the waitress had just deposited huge plates of scrambled eggs and home fries in front of us. "If he knew about this thing with Derek, or with *anybody*, he'd go berserk."

Aidan nodded. "He wants you to be his little girl, and not grow up."

"Which is not really an option." I squirted ketchup on my home fries and dug into them. "But don't change the subject. I want to know why you have to leave Hammond just because Rags recognized you. Because he might tell somebody? Why would it be such a big deal if your mother or sister found out you were here?"

He was peppering his eggs black. "Because they might think they should try to see me—which would be bad. I want them to think I just disappeared."

"Don't you think they've tried to find you?"

"I doubt it."

"Because your sister thinks the accident was your fault?"

He stopped chewing and stared at his plate. "It *was* my fault—that's one thing we agree on."

"But Rags said . . ."

"Piper, I told you, I don't want to talk about the accident. Please!"

I was afraid he wouldn't be able to eat anything else if I didn't agree. "Okay. Just tell me about your mother and your sister then."

He scooted a potato around on his plate until it fell off the edge. "They hate me. Not that I expect them to forgive and forget something like this. They can't get over it, and I don't blame them for that. But my sister wanted me to go to jail. And my mother . . . well, she's even worse."

"Worse how?"

"Can't stand to have me around. Can't stand to look at me. Before I left, she would cry whenever I walked into the room. That was harder to take than my sister screaming at me all the time. Obviously, I couldn't stay there."

"But that was more than a year ago. Maybe they feel differently now. Maybe they want you to come back."

He shook his head. "Believe me, they don't. My sister was so miserable she left her husband and moved back in with Mom. Maybe they can help each other get better, but not if I'm around. I have to stay away."

"But you go back there sometimes, don't you? That's where you go when you walk to Barlow." It didn't take a genius to figure that out.

He nodded.

"So, do you ever see them?"

My breakfast was gone, but Aidan was still picking at his. "I don't see them, but I check on them. I make sure both of their cars are still there; sometimes I check the mail or look in a window if I know they're gone. I want to make sure they're okay, you know? That they aren't *completely* ruined."

Like you are, I thought.

"Don't you think they'd at least want to know you're all right?"

A shrug. "I don't think so."

"Aidan . . . can I call you Aidan? I like knowing your real name."

Another shrug. "I guess so."

"Well, Aidan, for one thing, you have to stop shrugging all the time, like nothing matters."

He let his fork slip through his fingers. "Piper, nothing *does* matter anymore. Not really."

I banged my fist on the edge of the table. "That's ridiculous! As long as you're alive, things matter!"

The look he gave me raised goose bumps on my goose bumps. *As long as you're alive.* Why had I said that? It was probably something he thought about. It was probably something he thought about *a lot*.

"You have to stop blaming yourself for this, Aidan. It doesn't help anybody. Even if your sister can't forgive you, you should forgive yourself."

"Impossible," he said, wiping his hands on a napkin. "Let's pay the bill and get going, okay? I have a lot of walking to do today." He reached in his pocket and brought out a ten-dollar bill.

"I told you I'm paying for breakfast. You'll need your money if you don't have a job for a while."

He nodded and put the ten back in his pocket. "True. Thanks."

I picked up the check and headed toward the cash register. "I wish you were thanking me for something more important than breakfast," I said.

As he passed behind me, garbage bag at his side, his cheek brushed mine and he whispered in my ear, "I am."

By the time we got out to Route 7, it was almost ten o'clock. Traffic wasn't heavy, but cars came fast when they did come, so we stayed off the pavement.

"We're heading west?" I asked. "Away from the water? Won't you miss picking up shells at the beach?"

"There's farmland out here—I like that too. I'm thinking of going to Springhaven. You, however, should be heading home."

Suddenly I remembered Rachel. By now she'd certainly have woken up, found my note, seen the broken window, and freaked out. "Damn, I forgot to call home from the diner."

Aidan frowned. "Everybody will be worried about you, Piper. You have to go back."

"I will eventually—I just . . . I want to be with you for a while longer."

He switched the garbage bag to his other hand so he could intertwine his fingers with mine. "Okay. Just a little farther. There's a restaurant about a mile from here. You can call home from there, and they can come pick you up."

Between here and the restaurant would be nothing but

open fields. Between here and Springhaven not much more. "If you hitchhiked, you'd get there faster."

"No thanks. I'll get there walking."

"Aren't you *ever* going to get in a car again?"

He shrugged, then realized what he'd done. "Not if I can help it."

"I just can't imagine that. I mean, that would be like me saying I'll never have sex with anybody again."

He laughed, a reaction I was beginning to live for. "How are the two things in any way related?"

"They're totally related. Don't you think I feel guilty? I put my family in jeopardy just because I was stupid enough to give head to every guy who rubbed up against me. Now there's a maniac throwing rocks through my window. So, I could look at that evidence and say, 'No more sex for me—celibate for life!' But does that make sense?"

He shook his head. "Piper, you didn't . . . nobody died because of you."

I squeezed his hand. "I know. You hurt a lot of people. But not because you wanted to. You have to figure out a way to get over it."

He sighed, but didn't reply. We walked along quietly until a pickup truck passed us, braked heavily, and pulled off the road just up the highway.

"I guess he thinks we want a ride," I said.

The driver's door creaked open, and the guy jumped down, turned to us, and waved. "Hi there, Sandy! Just who I was looking for!"

Derek.

"It's him!" I said, pulling on Aidan's hand. "Run!"

Aidan dropped the bag and we started to run, but there was nowhere to go except into the weedy field, and you couldn't run fast there. Derek was on us in a minute. Or rather, he was on me.

I knew Derek was tall, but now rage, or insanity, or whatever had him by the throat made him seem enormous. He grabbed me away from Aidan's side and shook me so my head bobbled like one of those dolls you put in the back window of your car.

"Well, isn't this lucky? I wasn't even looking for you, and here you are, middle of nowhere just waiting for me." Derek said, grinning hugely with his horsey teeth.

Aidan tried to step between us, like he'd done with Andrew the day I'd met him in the park, but Derek shot out his arm and pushed Aidan down in the weeds. Aidan jumped up again quickly and stood a few feet away from us, looking stunned, like he didn't know what to do next.

"Let me go!" I wrenched myself away from Derek and stood with my hands on my hips so he couldn't see how much they were shaking. I decided it was better not to act scared. Any car whizzing past wasn't likely to notice us off in the field, and nobody would hear me if I started yelling. Bluffing seemed the best tactic.

"What's wrong with you, Derek?"

He grinned and shook his head. "If I was a whore like you, I wouldn't go around asking other people that question."

I held my hand flat and slapped him in the face. His expression didn't change, but he put his big paw up and felt the red shadow my smack had left. "Aren't we brave?"

Not really, no, but I kept up the act, even though my heart

felt ready to burst out of my chest. "First you stone my cat, then you hurt my sister, then you break a window in my house, and now *I'm next?* What are you doing this for?"

"I'm teaching you a lesson you'll never forget, slut. You need to remember: *You're not in charge*. You don't decide when the thing's over. You can't wiggle your tits in my face, and then the next day take off with some asshole like Andrew or this skank here," he said, motioning to Aidan, who seemed to be backing off a little.

"I thought Andrew was your friend."

"I don't have any friends."

"Gee, I wonder why."

I didn't even see the punch coming; it was so fast. Not a slap, but a fist, square in the middle of my face. I went down like a rag doll.

"You want to watch that nasty mouth of yours," Derek said.

It took me a minute to realize that the blood that was splattering my shirt was coming from my nose. My lip seemed to be split open too, but oddly nothing hurt. A neon sign was flashing in my brain, saying, *Get out of here, girl; get out now!*

From my spot in the weeds I saw Aidan come flying at Derek like a football tackle, but Derek took the blow easily and flipped Aidan over on his back.

"God, what a pussy . . . ," Derek began, but Aidan grabbed him around the legs and managed to unbalance him this time. Then they were both on the ground, rolling around and fighting.

I knew Aidan wouldn't be able to hold his own with Derek for long. Derek outweighed him by probably fifty pounds, and he had all that adrenaline fury going for him too. I couldn't let Aidan get hurt on my account.

I got to my feet slowly, feeling dizzy and nauseated. "Derek!" I shouted. "Leave him alone! You came to hurt *me*, remember? I'm over here!" I started to run a little then, so he'd have to leave Aidan to get me. But of course he couldn't just let Aidan go. He had to prove what a despicable punk he was, so he brought his right arm back as far as he could, then thrust his fist forward into Aidan's head, catching him right above the ear. Aidan groaned as he sank down in the dirt.

"I think that'll hold him long enough," Derek said.

Then I did run, but my head was so messed up I could tell I was running crooked. It didn't take Derek a minute to catch up to me. He grabbed hold of my upper arms, wrapped one leg around the back of my knees, and pulled my legs right out from under me. Before I knew it, I was lying on the ground with him on top of me.

"Now we're going to do it my way, Sandy. Whether you like it or not."

I was caught tight between his knees as he struggled with the zipper on his jeans.

"Derek, don't do this," I begged. Forget being fearless—it was time to plead. "This is rape. If you do this, you'll be *raping* me. Please, Derek!"

"Sandy, who's gonna believe I raped you? A girl with your reputation."

"Aidan will believe me!"

"Who? That guy? He's out cold. Besides, nobody knows him—he's a weirdo."

"Please, Derek! I've never . . . I'm, I'm a virgin."

He laughed. "Yeah, right. Me too." He held me down with a beefy arm, while he scooted his pants and boxers down to his knees. "Gimme a kiss, Sandy, just to get things rolling."

His face pushed into mine, and he chewed my bloody lip while he pressed my body flat to the ground. I tried to call out, to push him away, but he was immovable and I could barely breath under his weight, so I gave up and let my mind float away. I didn't try to, but I guess it was the only way I could escape what was happening to me. I knew he was unzipping my jeans, pushing down my underpants, but I knew it from a distance, like I was watching an awful movie. I heard him breathing heavily, but when I closed my eyes, I couldn't see his snarling face. I was going off somewhere and leaving my body behind.

"Ugh." Suddenly Derek stopped moving and fell against me with all his weight. His big chin banged into my nose, and I wanted to scream with the pain, but I didn't. I opened my eyes a crack. Maybe it was over.

Aidan was crouched down beside me, pushing at Derek until he managed to roll him off me. Derek lay on the ground on his back, eyes closed, mouth open, blood leaking out of a gash on his head.

Aidan helped me sit up and pull my clothes back together. He wiped my face with his shirt. "We have to get out of here before he wakes up."

"What—?" I couldn't make sense out of anything.

"I hit him with a jack I found in his truck. The keys are in the ignition, but we need to go *now*."

I staggered to my feet and tried to zip my pants. Aidan half led, half carried me to the pickup, and then pushed me up into the passenger seat. He ran back for his garbage bag, and I watched him take a last glance at Derek.

The truck started right up, but Aidan sat there for a minute, in the driver's seat, his hands on the steering wheel; he was breathing heavily. He adjusted the rearview mirror and looked into it for what seemed like a long time. Then with a leap we were on the highway, heading back toward Hammond.

"You're driving," I whispered, partly because I was amazed, and partly because my voice seemed to have left me when my mind did, back there in the field.

"I'm taking you to the hospital," he said, his hands locked in a death grip on the wheel.

"I'm okay," I said, although at that point I had no idea *what* I was.

"No, you aren't. You need to see a doctor. I don't know . . . what he did to you."

I put my hand up to my face and felt the drying blood. I must have looked like an escapee from a horror movie. Then I noticed Aidan's ear.

"There's blood coming from your ear," I said. "Where he hit you."

He brushed at it. "I'm fine. I'm going to get you into the hospital, and then . . . I think I better take the truck out of town, though I hate to. I'll leave it somewhere outside Snowden, and then I'll walk to Springhaven."

"But you need to see a doctor too." I was beginning to come to my senses. "You can't leave before you see a doctor."

"I can't do that, Piper."

"Why not?"

He glanced at me quickly. "What if I killed him? He wasn't moving. I just wanted to get him off you—I didn't mean to hit him that hard, but—"

"You *didn't*. Besides, you saved my life, Aidan. You saved me!"

"I don't think that's how the police will see it. I've done this kind of thing before, you know."

"You've done what before? Fought with a crazy person? Knocked out a rapist?" Just saying the word brought it all back to me. That's what had happened. Derek had tried to rape me. He'd tried, but had he done it? I put my hands on my belly. I hadn't been paying attention—I'd let my mind leave the premises. Which was scary all by itself.

We pulled up at the emergency room entrance and parked the truck with the dispute unresolved.

"Don't you see, Piper? I'd have to give my name—they might want to call my mother—this could get bad. The police will be called in—"

"I won't go in without you! I will not go in! You saved my life—you're not going to run off someplace with a bloody ear and a guilty conscience! I won't let you!"

He came around and opened the door, helped me out. By then I probably could have walked into the emergency room on my own, but I loved feeling Aidan's arm around my waist. He had not deserted me. I laid my sore cheek on his shoulder.

"Thank you," I said. "Thank you for being here."

We walked right up to the woman at the intake desk. Unshockable, she looked up at our bloody faces and said, "Looks like you've had an accident."

"Not exactly," I said. "We were beaten up."

"Beaten up," she repeated.

"We need a doctor, and we also need to talk . . . to the police," Aidan said.

"Your names?" the woman asked, her pen poised over a sheet of paper.

"Piper Ragsdale," I said.

He paused, then sighed heavily as he gave up his secret.

"Aidan Blankenship."

The Love Song of Piper H. Ragsdale
(with apologies to T. S. Eliot)

Let us go then, you and I,
When the morning mist is our ally,
And leave our parents, dead, divorced,
Or endlessly depressed, behind us.
Let us go with the intent
Of disallowing accidental blows
To make us life's no-shows.
I will not ask you, 'Do you?'
It matters only that *I* do.

In the room the doctors come and go,
Talking of scars and vertigo.

From the first I wondered, Do I dare?
If I touch you, will you scare?
I told you my mistakes, never guessing
Your nightmares. Will there be time
For the hundred questions
I cannot put in rhyme?
Now we've seen each other bleed—
Is there time for you and me?

Do I dare
Disturb the universe?
If I could erase one moment's pain
For the decision you cannot reverse,
I would.

—Piper Ragsdale

Chapter SEVENTEEN

There was only a curtain between Aidan and me in the ER so I could hear what he was telling the policewoman.

"I thought he was raping her, so I ran to his truck and found a jack—"

"He *was* trying to rape me!" I yelled from my cubicle. Yelling hurt, so I held the frigid ice pack up to my face again.

"Wait your turn," the cop said to me. "So you got the jack out of his truck—"

"Yeah. And I hit him with it. I'd already tried fighting with him, but he's stronger than I am. It was the only thing I could think of to do."

"So, this Derek, you knocked him out?"

"Yeah."

"And stole his truck?"

"I had to get Piper to the hospital!"

"We had to get away!" I threw in. "This guy is dangerous!"

She ignored me this time and made a call to somebody who must have been out looking for Derek. "Route 7 near Briar Road. Possible head injury," she said into her walkie-talkie.

Then she came to my side of the curtain. She read my name off her pad; then she looked up at me and frowned. "Did Derek do that to your face?"

I nodded. "He punched me. It's not broken though—the doctor said I was lucky." My voice sounded weird because my nose was packed with stuff to stop the bleeding. I was still going to need a few stitches in the corner of my mouth too. Wasn't looking forward to that, although my lip was so swollen I felt like I was already talking through Novocain.

"Hmmm. You don't look like you were lucky. Start by telling me what you and Aidan were doing walking along the highway."

I could almost feel him tense up next door. I wasn't going to rat him out. "Just walking. Aidan loves to walk."

"There's a trash bag full of clothes and sheets out in the truck. Who does that belong to?"

I shrugged the famous Aidan shrug. "Not me. Maybe Derek was taking the stuff to Goodwill or something."

"Uh-huh." She wrote something down on her pad of paper—it was hard to tell if she bought the Goodwill story or not. "And you'd been threatened by this Derek before, is that right?"

Now we were on the right track. "Yeah. He's been doing weird, scary stuff to my family for weeks, and then last night he threw a rock through a window of my house. The note on the rock said, 'It's your turn now, Sandy. See you soon.'"

"Is Derek an ex-boyfriend?" she asked.

I realized that was the simple explanation and I took it. "Sort of. Yes."

"And he's jealous that you're going with Aidan now?"

"I guess so." If she wanted to put us into neat categories that fit the story in her head, it seemed easier to go along with it.

She lowered her voice. "And you're not sure if he actually raped you or not, is that right?"

"He tried to, but I kind of . . . I don't know . . . I'm not sure." God, I felt stupid. What kind of idiot doesn't even know if she's been raped?

A nurse came through the curtain. "I'm just about to check her," she told the policewoman. "If you'll step outside a minute."

The cop went through the curtain while the nurse made me lie back on the table and put my knees up. I already had on one of those hospital johnnies that barely covers your body anyway, so I was now open for viewing. When she gently pushed my knees apart, I started to shake.

"Try to relax, honey," she said. "This won't take long."

There was a firm pressure as she pushed the speculum inside me. I couldn't really tell what was going on down there, but it didn't hurt. As promised, she removed everything quickly and let me sit up. I saw that she'd taken a swab of some kind, and put it in a plastic tube, and then sealed it up.

She called the policewoman back inside, then said to me, "You weren't penetrated. Your hymen isn't broken. I took a swab sample to see if there was any semen inside you." She turned to the cop. "In case you need the information later." The cop nodded.

My first reaction was relief. Derek hadn't raped me. Aidan had stopped him. This time he really *was* my superhero! But then I thought, if he hadn't actually raped me, did that mean

Aidan might be in trouble? How could we *prove* that Derek was trying to rape me? Unless there was something on that swab!

"I called your father and your sisters at the numbers you gave me," the policewoman said. "I had to leave a message for your dad, but your sisters are on their way."

"Thanks." *Great*. At least I wouldn't have to face Rags immediately. He was no doubt spending the day with the lovely Laura King.

Because he was eighteen, Aidan hadn't had to give the policewoman his mother's name. He just told her his father was dead and his mother didn't live nearby. He was relieved about that, at least.

There was a doctor in with Aidan while the nurse stitched up my mouth. She numbed it first, but I closed my eyes anyway. "By tomorrow you're going to be black-and-blue, and your face is gonna hurt like the dickens. We'll get you a prescription to help with that."

Right about then, Rachel and Daisy arrived at my little curtained room. Daisy started to cry as soon as she saw me.

"It's okay, Daise," I said. "It doesn't hurt that much." She took my hand, but looked at the floor and made little mewing noises as the tears fell.

"I was so scared when I got your note and then saw the living room," Rachel said. For the first time since I'd met her, her hair was stringy and uncombed, her clothing mismatched. "I knew something bad was going on. It was Derek, wasn't it?"

I nodded. Daisy cried harder.

"I knew it," Rachel said. "I should have called your dad right away, but I didn't want to worry him if you were really coming right back."

"He probably wasn't home anyway. I'm sorry, Rachel. I should have called you. I meant to call you—"

"I'm just glad you're all right—you are, aren't you? Your face is pretty messed up— that sergeant person who called didn't say too much—just that you'd been hurt while you were walking on the highway—but I knew it must have had something to do with that guy Derek. Why were you walking on the highway? Did he hit you in the face?" Rachel was so agitated, I could barely get a word in edgewise.

"I was walking with Aidan—"

"Aidan? Who's Aidan?"

"You know . . . my friend, Walker. Aidan is his real name."

"It is?"

"I'll explain later. Anyway, we were walking, and Derek drove by in the truck and saw us. He was furious. He hit me, and then he hit Aidan, and then he . . . he tried to rape me."

Daisy drew in her breath. "No!"

"It's okay," I said, squeezing her hand. "He didn't do it. Aidan got a jack from Derek's truck and hit him with it. He knocked him out. And then we came here in the truck." I'd left out a few details, but they got the gist of it.

"Where is Aidan now?" Rachel asked.

I pointed to the curtain, and then called to him. "Are you okay, Aidan?"

"Yeah," he said, but his voice sounded far away and odd.

The doctor parted the curtain between us. "We're going to have to admit your friend. I'm afraid he has a concussion, and I want to keep an eye on him for a day or two. If he lived with someone, I might let him go, but I'm not sending him home alone in this condition."

Home? Aidan didn't even have a home. I could see him lying back on the table, looking a lot less energetic than when he'd helped me into the hospital. "You don't look so good," I said.

"Headache," was all he said.

I looked at the doctor. "But he was okay before!"

"Adrenaline. You'll crash too."

"He can come home with us," I said. "We can watch him tonight."

"Well, *you* can't," the doctor said. "You need to rest. It's better that he stays here so your family can look after you."

"But he saved my life!" I said. "We can't leave him in the hospital!"

"It's okay, Piper," Aidan whispered. "Go home. I'm okay."

By the time Rags got there, I was already signed out and ready to leave. Aidan was going to be moved upstairs as soon as they had a bed ready. He was so groggy I didn't try to talk to him again.

I guess my face wasn't waiting until tomorrow to turn black-and-blue. Rags took one look at me and just about fell over. "What the hell happened? My God, the first day your mother's gone and you get beaten to a pulp!"

Fortunately, Rachel and the by-now-recovered Daisy were happy to retell the saga of my morning. Since it all seemed to be turning out okay, they were kind of excited to be part of the drama. But now I was starting to worry. What if Aidan *wasn't* okay? Or what if Derek was seriously injured, or worse? Or what if Derek was okay, but he told horrible lies about what happened? Did I really think there was any chance he'd tell the truth?

By the time we all got back to the house, Rags was in a state. Somehow we'd forgotten to tell him about the broken window—entering a living room filled with shattered glass had him walking around in shocked circles for a few minutes. I wondered how long it would be until I had to come clean with the details.

"I don't know if I should call Colleen and Nathan or not," he said. "You're apparently all right now—even though you look like hell—and this is an awfully upsetting thing to find out on the first day of your honeymoon. But if I don't call, I know your mother will be upset that I didn't."

"How about waiting until tomorrow?" I said. "Then you can downplay the whole thing and tell her I'm fine. Tomorrow is plenty of time."

Rags opened his mouth like he wanted to bite me, but then he looked at Daisy, who'd already used up a tree's worth of tissues, and changed his expression. "You know what? How about if you and Rachel go out and get us something to eat?" He pulled some bills from his pocket. "Maybe some ribs from that barbecue place by the mall."

"You're hungry?" Daisy said. "I feel sort of nauseated myself."

"You don't have to get ribs then. Get some hot-and-sour soup at the Chinese place. That's good for an iffy stomach."

Clearly he just wanted Daisy gone, and Rachel figured that out. "Yeah, let's go get some Chinese, Daisy. I forgot to thaw out the stuff your mom left in the freezer anyway."

Daisy probably knew what was up too, but she followed Rachel out the door. The kid was doing a lot of growing up this summer.

As soon as they were gone, Rags sat down on a chair across

from where I was lying on the couch, the blue ice bag draped over my nose. "If you have an idea about how to downplay the fact that you were beaten and nearly raped this morning, I'd like to know what it is."

"Dad—"

"Because this is not downplayable, Piper! This is horrible! *Horrible!* Your mother is going to . . ." Suddenly he couldn't speak, although his mouth was still hanging open as if it were looking for more words. When the tears began to roll out of his eyes, I could only stare. Rags crying? *Never.* And yet it was undeniable.

"Dad, I'm okay," I said. "Nothing happened."

"Plenty happened!" he barked through his tears. "My daughter, my first child, my *baby* has been beaten up! This is my nightmare, Sandpiper! This is why I didn't want you walking around in those tight little tops, flaunting yourself. . . ." He shook his head and tried to pull himself together, fished a handkerchief out of his pocket to wipe his face. "Oh, what's the use? You're so scornful of me. And now this has happened." He blew his nose and sighed.

"Dad, this had nothing to do with the clothes I wear, believe me."

"Well, what *did* it have to do with? You knew this boy, didn't you? Was it one of those boys I saw you with downtown? I knew they looked like trouble, but I never expected something like *this*."

What choice did I have? I'd have to tell it all sooner or later anyway. I took a deep breath and jumped in. "He was mad at me. Derek. Because I was . . . we used to . . . sort of . . . have oral sex. . . for a while."

Rags looked at me as though I was suddenly speaking a foreign language. He cocked his ear at me, like he hadn't heard me correctly, but I knew he had.

I dropped the blue bag on the floor. "He wanted me to have, you know, regular sex with him too. But I didn't want to—I didn't really like him that much. So I stopped seeing him and started seeing another guy, a friend of his. I didn't realize how mad he was about it. I don't think he's a normal person. A normal person wouldn't—"

"Was his friend Aidan?" Rags was trying to put the pieces together.

"No! Andrew. You don't know him."

"But you aren't seeing *Andrew* anymore either?"

"Right."

"Now you're seeing Aidan?"

"Not exactly. I mean, we're friends, but—"

"Piper, how many boys have you had sex with?"

I shrugged. "A few. Maybe . . . ten. Just oral sex though, not real sex. I'm a virgin!"

Rags stared at me for a minute, as if I were changing color right in front of him. Then he closed his eyes and said, "Dear Lord."

"Dad—"

"Oral sex *is* real sex!" he shouted, jumping up. He stalked around the room trying to calm himself down. "Piper, having sex with someone is a very intimate act—you don't do it with everybody you meet, with people you don't even 'like that much'!"

I didn't have to say it. I just looked at him hard and he got it. For a change, he really *got* it.

"You think *I* have sex with everybody I meet?" he asked.

"Well, every woman between twenty-five and forty-five anyway."

"Oh, Piper." He dropped back into the chair and put his head into his hands. "So, you're saying this is my fault? You're following my lead?"

"I'm saying you have no right to tell me not to do what you do."

His head swung up and he glared at me. "I have every right! I'm your father and you're not even sixteen yet!"

That hit a nerve. "You don't *act* like my father! You only come to see me when Colleen guilt-trips you into it! You don't even like me now that I'm not your little *baby* anymore!" This outburst tripped my own sprinkler system, and I started to bawl. The whole awfulness of the day sank down onto my shoulders, and I beat the couch cushions with my fists as I cried. The more I cried, the more my nose hurt, but I couldn't seem to stop.

Rags scooted me up on the couch and sat next to me with his arms around me so I was crying into his shirt. "Sandpiper, that's not true! Of course I still love you. You're my daughter—I'll always love you."

"You don't act like it!" I said through my sobs. I was so mad at him, but at the same time it was wonderful to be able to lean against him and cry. To be his baby again.

"Shh, sweetheart. I'm sorry. I'm so sorry if you think that's true. I admit it's been harder for me since you've . . . matured. I guess I don't know how to be a father to a young woman. Obviously I'm doing a lousy job of it."

"Just because I've changed outside doesn't mean I'm different inside," I said. "I . . . I miss you!"

He hugged me so tightly then it hurt my face, but I didn't complain. We sat together on the couch, not saying much, calming each other down, until we heard the car in the driveway. Rags got up to open the door for Rachel and Daisy.

They walked in with four brown bags that smelled of delicious sauces. We wouldn't have to cook all week.

"You know, Dad," Daisy said on her way into the kitchen, "you should probably call Grandma Edie and tell her what happened."

Rags groaned, then turned to me with a half smile. "We'll call her tomorrow. Tomorrow is plenty of time."

Lucky

Lucky
you didn't break my nose,
only cracked my lip,
bloodied my clothes.

Lucky
I wasn't walking alone
when you showed up
with your knucklebone.

Lucky
I was temporarily missing
when you unzipped your pants,
then insisted on mine.

Lucky
you missed your chance
to split me and run.
Lucky for you I had no gun.

Luck, karma, blessing,
catching a break.
You were the lucky one,
my biggest mistake.

—*Piper Ragsdale*

Chapter EIGHTEEN

Derek was alive. The police sergeant called after
dinner and talked to Rags. I guess it was good news, at least as
far as Aidan was concerned, but personally I wouldn't have
missed the guy. He was standing up and walking around in the
field when they found him, cursing like a pirate, the cop said.
They took him to the hospital first, to get his head sewn up,
and then into custody at the station.

The reason they were calling us was to ask if I wanted to
press charges against him. I wanted to use him for a dartboard
or make him walk the plank, but pressing charges would have
to satisfy me. I went up to bed after that and didn't find out
until the next morning that Rags, feeling guilty and uncertain,
had called both Edie and Colleen after all.

I woke up with a hot poker stuck in the middle of my face
where my nose had once been. The mirror revealed the truth:
everything from my nose to my left ear, and from my left eye-
brow to my chin was a dark angry purple, which would have
coordinated nicely with my lavender bridesmaid's dress. The
nose itself was twice the size it should have been, my left eye

was swollen shut, and all of it hurt like hell.

Rags was still asleep on the living room couch when I staggered downstairs—I noticed he'd boarded over the window and swept up the glass. Edie had apparently arrived early and was mixing eggs in the kitchen.

The usual stern look she gave everybody melted like that *Scream* painting when she saw me. "Good Lord in heaven! What did he *do* to you?!" She took me by the shoulders, sat me on a stool, and examined my bruises. "That bastard!" she said in her coldest voice.

"It hurts," I said, and talking made it hurt more. "Do you know where Rags put the pain pills?"

"Right here," she said, picking up the little brown bottle of relief from the counter. She poured me a glass of water and handed me one pill. "I'd give you juice, but I'm afraid the acid would hurt your mouth."

"Okay." I was willing to do as I was told today. I just wanted to stop feeling terrible. Looking terrible I couldn't do much about.

"I'm making you eggs with cheese. You need protein to heal yourself. Do you drink milk?"

"Not crazy about it," I said.

"Me either. How about if I put chocolate syrup in it?"

"Okay." I tried to smile with the good side of my lip. It occurred to me I'd never actually seen Edie cook anything. "Thanks, Grandma."

She waved away my thanks. "Least I can do, under the circumstances." She scooped my scrambled eggs onto a plate, and the cheese strings swirled out of the pan. Yum.

"Did Rags tell you everything?" I asked her.

"He told me more than I ever wanted to hear about one of my granddaughters. He called your mother and Nathan last night too, which I think was the right thing to do, honeymoon or not."

"They aren't coming home, are they?"

"I don't think so. Your mother will call you this morning. We were all on the phone back and forth last night for a long time. I think Adrienne finally convinced them that you were all right, and that there were plenty of people back here to watch over the three of you."

"Adrienne? How did she get involved?"

"I called her," Edie said. "She's closer to your mother than anybody else, including me, and I thought she ought to talk to her. Glad I did. She's a sensible woman, that Adrienne."

"I thought you didn't get along with her."

"Don't be ridiculous! I've known Adrienne since she was a young girl, and I've always liked her very much. I just wish she'd watch her weight. I know it's none of my business, but I hate to think of her spending her life alone, as I've had to."

How odd. I'd never heard Edie sound the least bit remorseful before. The few times I'd heard her mention my grandfather, who'd left her for a woman he met when he worked in Ohio one winter, she called him, 'That selfish jackass.' She'd never remarried. She started selling real estate and made quite a bit of money. I remember when Colleen and Rags were getting divorced, Edie tried to get Colleen to sell real estate too. "You can earn the same kind of living a man can. You'll never need to marry again!" she'd said. But Colleen stuck to dipping chocolates and stayed friends with her first husband, who introduced her to her second. People are different, even when they're related.

Edie sighed. "Your mother is fortunate in many ways. I wish I'd had such a loyal friend as Adrienne to follow me through my life."

"Me too," I said. "I thought I had one, but I guess it didn't last forever."

"Most things don't," Edie said, slipping back into her matter-of-fact attitude, setting the chocolate milk on the table. "Eat your eggs. I'm going to call Bill Baker down at the hardware store and see how soon he can get up here to replace that window."

By noon I'd talked to Colleen, Nathan, and Adrienne on the phone. Colleen was glad to hear my voice, she said. Did I want her to come back, because she absolutely would if I needed her, on the next plane. Which was nice to know. But I told her please not to wreck her honeymoon, that Rags had taken over the living room couch, Edie the kitchen, and all was well.

"Well, it can't be that good," she said. "Rags told me your face is the color of a ripe plum."

"Yeah. I'm going to press charges against the guy," I said.

There was a long silence on her end. "Piper, I've never even heard of this Derek person before. What's his last name? Have you known him very long?"

"Derek Murphy. I met him at school. It's not like he was a good friend or anything."

"I should hope not!" She sighed. "It's my fault. I was so busy with this wedding I wasn't paying enough attention to you lately. I knew there was something wrong, but it didn't occur to me that it was anything like this. That you even *knew* a boy like this Derek! And the other boy—Aidan—I've never heard of him either. It's like you've had a secret life!"

"It's not your fault, Mom. Really. It's . . . complicated. Can we talk about it when you get back?"

"Oh, we'll be talking about it for a long time to come, Piper. Of that you can be sure!"

Nathan got on for a few minutes. He wanted me to take down the name of a woman he knew who did rape counseling.

"Anne Jenkins at the Barlow Women's Clinic. She's very good. I think you should call her right away," he said.

"But I wasn't *raped*," I said. I couldn't believe I was having this conversation with my brand-new stepfather.

"Honey, believe me, you need to talk to a professional. Someone who deals with this all the time. You may be more traumatized than you realize."

Maybe he was right, but in a funny way I felt like I'd been more traumatized *before* all this happened. As if the whole thing with Derek was kind of a big storm—really scary, but at least it had blown away a lot of debris and cleaned the place up. I took down her name though and promised I'd call.

Then Adrienne phoned to say if I wanted to talk to any-body about what had happened, in the absence of my mother, she was ready and willing to be of service. I told her I didn't feel like going through it all again right now, but there was another way for her to help me out.

"Would you drive me down to the hospital this afternoon to see Aidan? I don't want to go with Rags, and Rachel is out somewhere."

"No problem. Can I actually meet him? I'd like to be able to report back to your mother if possible. She's very upset that she's never heard of either boy involved in this incident."

"You can meet him. Just remember, Aidan is the *good* guy."

The surprise phone call came as I was waiting for Adrienne to pick me up. Edie had gone home for a while, and Rags was supervising the window repair, so I answered the phone.

"Is that you? Can you talk? Are you in pain?" It was Melissa. Apparently *everybody* liked you better once you'd had the crap beaten out of you.

"Yes to all three questions. I guess you heard what happened."

"God, Sandy, I'm so shocked! I knew Derek was kind of crazy, but I never thought he'd do something like *this!* Did he really try to rape you?"

"Yeah. It was pretty bad. How'd you hear about it?"

"My uncle's a policeman, remember? He called my mom."

"Oh, yeah, right."

There was some sighing on the line, and I had the feeling Melissa was trying to put something into words, but couldn't figure out how to do it.

"Are you trying to say, I told you so?"

"Sandy, *no!* I don't think that at all! Nobody deserves what Derek did to you! I just wanted to say . . . it was good to talk to you at the wedding the other day."

"Oh. Well, I was happy you came."

"And I'm glad Derek didn't hurt you any worse than he did."

"Yeah, me too."

"Anyway, I have to go, but maybe we could hang out again sometime?"

"That'd be good."

"I mean, jeez, you're, like, my oldest friend!" She said in a voice that sounded as if she really was.

I wondered why she wanted to revive a friendship I thought she'd already buried. Was it because my attack was going to make me a semicelebrity in town? I hoped that wasn't it. Maybe she'd just realized how upset she would have been if Derek's attack hadn't been stopped before he was through with me. That was an option I could live with.

Adrienne gave me a big hug as soon as she came into the house, and it surprised me how much I seemed to need it. For a change I wasn't the first one to let go. She'd brought over some makeup to cover my bruises, and we sat on my bed while she applied it. Dabbing on the tan goo seemed to buoy her spirits, but I can't say it did much for my face.

On the drive to the hospital she asked me how I'd met Aidan and how well I knew him.

"I've really only known him three or four weeks, I guess. But I feel like I know him pretty well. I mean, better than most people."

She looked over at me. "Does that mean you . . . like him a lot?"

I nodded, and Adrienne nodded back; she knew what I meant.

"Rags told me about the accident, how Aidan ran over his nephew. It's so terrible. That couldn't be an easy thing to get over."

"He isn't over it. Nobody in his family is over it. That's why he doesn't live with them anymore. His sister hates him, and his mother cries every time he walks in the room. His dad died when he was seven." Somehow it seemed okay to tell Adrienne this stuff.

"That's just awful. God, that poor kid. Don't worry, Piper, we'll take care of him. Nathan can set him up with a therapist when he gets back."

"Aidan doesn't have much money. Besides, he won't talk to *anybody* about the accident."

"Which is why he needs to—you can't keep something like that bottled up inside you. The guilt he feels must be horrible. And he doesn't even have parents to help him get through it. Nathan will help figure out the money part. Somebody will see him."

I was amazed at the way my family and friends were rallying around not only me, but Aidan too. No doubt I still had some explaining to do, but so far no one had said what I'd been thinking, which was: *You asked for this, you tramp.* They didn't say it, and I don't think they thought it either.

Before we got to the hospital, I actually felt normal enough to ask Adrienne a question that had nothing to do with my own life.

"Did you like Gil Steinhart? I thought he was *so* nice."

Adrienne smiled. "He said the same thing about you."

"He did?"

"Yup. And I think he kinda likes me too. And the feeling is mutual."

"That's so great!" I said.

"I'm planning to go out to California the week before school starts so he can show me around San Francisco," she said, blushing. "I'm trying not to get my hopes up too much, but . . . dammit, I really like Gil, and I plan on doing whatever it takes to make him see I'm too good to pass up!"

"You are, Adrienne," I told her. "You definitely are."

* * *

Aidan was sitting up in bed staring at a game show when we came in. I think he was embarrassed to be caught watching the tube.

"I haven't seen TV in so long," he said as he flicked it off.

I introduced him to Adrienne, and she immediately took his hand and said, "I wanted to thank you in person for what you did for Piper. You're very brave. We all owe you a big debt of gratitude."

And then another odd thing happened: Aidan's eyes filled with tears.

Adrienne kept talking in that same soothing voice I'd heard her use with the little kids in her class. "I know your whole story—you don't have to say a thing. We're going to help you however we can. We're taking care of you now—don't you worry."

Aidan blinked back as much of the salt water as he could, but he also smiled. A sad smile, but still a smile.

I sat carefully on the bed. "How's your head? Does it hurt?"

"I'm okay. Look at you though," he said, putting a hand up to my cheek. "Makes me wish I'd hit him harder."

"Yeah, although I guess I'm glad he isn't dead. Can you get out of here today?"

He shook his head. "I shouldn't have told that doctor I live alone. He doesn't want me staying by myself, which means I have to stay in *here*."

"So, if you had someplace to stay, somebody to watch you, he'd let you out?" Adrienne said.

"I think so."

I was trying to figure out how I was going to talk Rags and Edie into letting Aidan stay in Colleen and Nathan's bedroom for a few days, but Adrienne was way ahead of me.

"Well, if that's the only problem, you can come and stay in my guest room. There's a nice big TV in there, and anyway a kindergarten teacher is the next best thing to a nurse, you know."

"Really? You mean it?" I asked.

"Of course I mean it. What's your doctor's name, Aidan? I'll go track him down."

Which she did. By the time visiting hours were over, Aidan was free. Sort of. The doctor had a hundred rules.

"I want you sitting or lying down. As little walking around as possible for at least another twenty-four hours. Pills no more than four a day, one every six hours. Eat lightly. If you feel dizzy or nauseous, or if your vision blurs, you call the hospital and have me paged. And Ms.—?"

"Just call me Adrienne."

"Adrienne, you need to change that bandage in the morning for two more days. Then if there's no drainage it can stay off. I'll need your phone number so I can check in with Aidan tomorrow."

"I never mind giving my phone number to a handsome man," she said with a laugh as she wrote the number on his pad. The doctor blushed.

Huh! I'd never seen Adrienne act so flirtatious before. I had a feeling it was because she knew Gil liked her a lot. It's funny how knowing that one person cares about you makes you able to like yourself better too.

I wanted to go over to Adrienne's to help get Aidan settled

in, but my face was starting to hurt again and I knew I needed another pain pill. He was getting tired anyway, he said, so I promised to come over first thing in the morning. Adrienne only lives about six blocks away, so I can walk there easily.

I ran into the house, then stopped dead in my tracks. Something *else* was wrong. Rags, Edie, and Rachel were all clustered around Daisy who was sitting on the sofa, sobbing hysterically.

"*Now* what happened?" I asked.

The three noncrying people looked up at me.

"Daisy broke up with Sam," Rachel said.

God, that was all? You'd think, after everything else that was going on, Daisy could have toned down the dramatics a little bit—after all, *she* broke up with *him*. At least she wasn't dumped. Maybe she was jealous of all the attention I was getting lately. Well, I could understand that.

"Gee, Daise," I said, "I'm sorry. If you liked him so much, why did you break up?"

She looked at me with fury in her eyes. "I told him . . ." she sputtered, "I told him about you."

"You did?"

Rachel put her arm around Daisy's shoulders.

"I hate him!" Daisy sobbed again. "I hate him!"

"Did he say something . . . ?" I asked, but I didn't really want to know.

"Yeah, he said something! He said a slut like you deserved whatever she got!"

A Slut Like Me

Strike one.
A plummy stain spreads across
my face, darker than grape juice.
He isn't done.

Strike two.
In the dirt he prepares me
for the screw. I think I'm saved!
Not true.

Strike three.
Word's out—I did him first.
Did I think I'd get off
scot-free?

You deserved it,
I said to myself, but it feels
worse to hear it from others.
A slut like me.

—*Piper Ragsdale*

Chapter NINETEEN

It was what I'd been waiting for somebody to say.

It's your own fault. It was what I'd been trying not to say to myself. And even though I hardly knew this Sam kid, his words stung like bees. He wasn't the only person who'd see it this way. My "reputation" had now become the latest news; in a day or two everybody I'd ever known would be discussing whether or not I was to blame for my own broken face. Some of them would probably agree with Sam—I *ought* to have been raped. I *deserved* it.

Daisy couldn't decide who to be more mad at, Sam or me. She'd obviously been mad enough at him to break up with him, but now she was mad at me for instigating the whole thing.

"Daisy stuck up for you, didn't you, Daise?" Rachel said.

I leaned against the wall. "You did?"

Daisy stared up at me with cold eyes and shaking lips. "You're my sister," she said. "I *had* to."

"And now you hate me, don't you?" I asked her.

"*Yes!*" she screamed at me, her face distorted. "*I do!*" Then she really sobbed, like the release valve inside her had let go completely. Rachel hugged her, but looked over at me sadly.

Rags got up and scratched his head. "Daisy, I know you feel that way now—"

"I *loved* Sam," she croaked.

Of course, Edie was the one to say what the rest of us were thinking. "Oh, for heaven's sake, Daisy, you're thirteen years old. You'll love again." She stood up. "I think we're all making far too much of this. I'm going to put Colleen's casserole in the oven and make a salad. Maybe I'll even make some biscuits. We need to start climbing out of this *hole*." She gave us all one of her looks before heading for the kitchen.

"Daisy, I'm really sorry about Sam," I said.

"No, you're not! You all think I'm being silly! I have feelings too, you know!" She got up and ran for the stairs, bawling all the way.

Rags sighed. "Well, I don't know what to do. I thought this *boyfriend* was just a kid thing. Obviously, I don't have a clue what's going on with either of my daughters. I'm going to take a walk and clear my head." He scooted out the front door before we could think of a reason to stop him.

Rachel pulled me down onto the couch next to her and leaned over, laying her head on my shoulder. "This should never have happened to you, Piper. Don't you believe for a second that it should have."

"It shouldn't have happened to Daisy either," I said.

"Daisy will get over it—don't worry about her right now. Worry about yourself."

I suddenly felt all my carefully erected barriers collapse under the floodwaters. I cried like a little kid, like a faucet without a shutoff valve, and Rachel held me tighter than you'd think a size two petite could hold you. When I finally dried up into leftover sniffles, I saw that she'd been leaking too. We both looked pretty bad, but I must have looked worse, weeping through my swollen, discolored eye. It made me laugh, and then she laughed too, and in a minute we were giddy, blowing our noses between attacks of nervous giggles.

We stopped abruptly when Rags came back in, flanked by two police officers—the woman sergeant from the hospital and a man.

"They just pulled up out front," Rags said. "Do you mind talking to them, Piper? I know it's been a tough day."

"It's okay," I said. "Can Rachel stay here?" She was holding on to my hand so hard that my fingers ached, but I wasn't about to tell her to let go.

The policewoman nodded. "Sure, we just have a few more questions for you."

"We've already talked to Aidan. The hospital gave us his new address," the second police officer said.

"What new address?" Rags wanted to know.

"Adrienne's house," I said. "She's letting him stay in her guest room."

"What? She doesn't even know him!"

"She knows *me*," I said, which pretty much shut him up.

"We need to go over a few of the facts you gave us earlier," the policewoman said. "You say you were walking along the highway when Derek's truck stopped in front of you, is that correct?"

"Right."

"And then what happened?"

I sighed and went through the whole story again, the same way I had before. She nodded. "And Derek used to be your boyfriend, but now Aidan is?"

I decided I'd better tell everything the way it really was. "Well . . . not exactly. I mean, I used to spend time with Derek, but I never really thought of him as my boyfriend."

"But he wanted to have sex with you?"

"Yeah. Well, we did some stuff, just not, you know, regular sex."

She nodded. "And Aidan?"

"He's my friend, my very good friend."

"And have you had any kind of sexual relations with him?"

"No! Not with Aidan!"

"You haven't?" Rags asked. "I assumed—"

"You assume too much, Dad."

The policewoman closed her book. "Well, I have to warn you; Derek Murphy tells a very different story."

"Oh, God, what does he say?"

"He says the three of you left Hammond together in his truck. That Aidan said he needed a ride to Barlow and he offered him one. He says you were already with him in the truck when he picked Aidan up."

"What? That's a total lie!"

She continued. "Then when you got out into the country, Aidan pulled a knife on him, made him pull the truck over and get out. He says Aidan was jealous because you'd had sex with him."

"He's lying!" I screamed. I was on my feet now, and Rachel was beside me. "Aidan doesn't even *have* a knife!"

"I'm just repeating his story. He says Aidan fought with

him and then hit him over the head with the jack."

We were all silent for a minute, stunned. Suddenly Rachel said, "Then how come Piper's face is all black-and-blue?"

"Yeah! What did he say about that?"

The officer sighed. "He said Aidan knocked you against the side of the truck. Again, out of jealousy."

"That is such bullshit!" I screamed again.

Rachel squeezed my hand even harder. "Nobody's going to believe him."

"What about that swab thing the nurse took? Couldn't that prove he tried to rape me?"

"It was negative for sperm. I'm afraid there will be a trial."

"A trial?"

"You're pressing charges against him, and he's denying the charges. Unless one of you changes your stories, we're going to trial."

"But just Derek and me, right?"

"And Aidan. We'll have to hear his side of things, especially now that Derek is accusing him."

"No!" I looked at Rags. "Aidan can't go through another trial. He can't!"

"Looks like he'll have to, baby," Rags said, coming up behind me and putting a hand on my shoulder.

This really *was* my fault. I'd gotten Aidan mixed up in this whole mess. How had this happened?

The officers left, and the three of us stood in the living room, staring at the carpet. After a minute Rachel hugged me and went upstairs to see how Daisy was doing. I'm sure she had no idea when she arrived here just how exhausting living with us would be.

Then it was just Rags and me. He didn't look like he was going to hug me again, which was just as well. I felt the same way about him that Daisy felt about me. There wasn't one particular thing I wanted to blame him for, but it seemed like my life would have been a lot easier if he'd just been a different kind of father. Someone who wasn't freaked out by his own kid's puberty. Someone who didn't change girlfriends as often as he changed his shirt. Someone who listened to me, who saw who I really was. Someone who trusted me. Still, he was my dad and, in spite of everything, I loved him. I just wasn't ready to leap into full forgiveness yet. I wasn't sure he even knew he needed it.

He sat down next to me, looking uncomfortable. "We need to talk about something."

What *now?*

"Maybe this isn't the best time for it—I was planning on telling everybody when Colleen and Nathan got back from their honeymoon, but I feel like I'm keeping a secret from you and Daisy if I don't tell you now. And I think there have been enough secrets in this family."

My heart practically stopped beating. I didn't know if I could take any more awful revelations.

"The thing is, Laura is a very good person, and I'm getting too old to keep running around like . . . well, like a kid. So, Laura and I are engaged, Piper. We're going to get married."

My jaw dropped so far it hurt my stitches. "Ow," I said, putting my hand to my mouth. "You're getting married? *You?*" But even as I said it, I realized I was expecting worse news.

"Piper, I know it's surprising, right after your mother's wedding and all, but I hope you'll get to know Laura and eventually like her the way you like Nathan."

"Who says I like Nathan?" Where were those pain pills?

"I know you like Nathan. I can tell."

I ran my hand over the nubbly couch pillow. "Does Laura King have any children?" I asked finally. For some reason it seemed like the only question that mattered.

Rags nodded. "She has a seven-year-old daughter. Her name is Emma."

Wouldn't you know? "Well, that's great for you, huh? You like *little* girls."

"Piper, she'll never be my daughter the way you and Daisy are."

"And she'll never be my sister the way Daisy and Rachel are." Which is something I hadn't known I felt until I said it out loud. Huh.

He nodded again. "That's okay. We can't force you to like each other, and we wouldn't try."

"Oh, you probably will sooner or later. I thought you said you'd never get married again."

He shrugged. "You change as you get older. The world changes you. I'm ready now."

"So I guess we're both growing up at the same time. That wasn't very good planning, was it?"

Rags smiled. "You're right. I'm sorry it took me so long."

Rachel appeared at the top of the stairs, hugging her sweater around her ribs. "Daisy wants you to come up to her room, Piper."

"Really? Is she going to hit me? I'm not sure I can take any more punches today."

Rachel smiled. "I don't think so. She just wants to talk."

SANDPIPER

I trudged upstairs, heavy with the news of more family expansion and not at all anxious to enter Daisy's room. Unless Rachel was a miracle worker, Daisy would want to chew over the whole incident again, and I just wasn't up to it. All I really wanted was to fall into bed and forget the last few days ever happened. But since that was impossible anyway, I might as well be a dutiful sister and let Daisy wail on me for a while. What choice did I have?

I knocked. "Daise, Rachel says you want to talk to me."

Daisy flung the door open in her usual theatrical way, then backed across the room as I entered.

"I know you don't believe me," I said, "but I really am sorry that you and Sam broke up over this."

She nodded. "That's what Rachel said."

"What else did Rachel say?" I was so exhausted I sank down onto Daisy's bed.

Daisy sighed and turned to stare out her window. "She said that it was cruel of Sam to say something so mean about you. That he didn't even know you. She said she was proud of me for standing up for you."

"Yeah, I'm surprised you did! I mean, I know you've been mad at me too, and I don't blame you. I really am sorry."

She turned back to me then, her eyes sparkling with tears again. "I couldn't believe Sam said that. If he saw what you look like. . . . You got beaten up and almost raped! How could you deserve that? You *didn't* deserve it."

I was beside her in a minute, arms around her skinny back. "Don't cry, Daise. It's over. I'm just glad Derek didn't hurt you any worse than he did."

"When you told me about Derek, I thought you were

exaggerating to scare me or something. I didn't think anybody I knew could be so . . . evil."

"I know," I said, pulling tissues from a nearby box, one for each of us.

She blew her nose. "I guess partly I'm mad at myself for falling for a guy like Sam who'd be such a jerk. And then not realizing that Derek was an even bigger one."

I wiped my eyes. "Sometimes it takes a while before you can tell the jerks from the good guys."

"Aidan is a good guy, isn't he?"

"Yeah, he is. Definitely."

"Do you love him?"

I nodded. "But I don't think he's ready to hear it yet."

"Why did something so awful have to happen to him?"

"I don't know." I pulled her down onto the bed beside me. "I know this though: now that I've seen a good guy up close, I'm not settling for jerks anymore. And I'm not going to *be* a jerk anymore either. I want to be the kind of person Aidan could love—someday."

Daisy smiled. "I bet you already are. I mean, look, I don't hate you anymore."

"Yeah, that was easier than I expected."

"Thank Rachel. She's good at explaining things."

I patted her hand and stood up. "I will. But first I have to go lie down for a while. My face hurts." But before I got to the door, I remembered the other news of the day.

"Hey, guess what Rags just told me? He's marrying Laura King, and we're going to have *another* sister."

Daisy's eyes widened. "Awesome!" she shrieked.

We're so different, you just have to laugh.

Chapter TWENTY

After an uncomfortable night—the pillow was too
hard for my nose, and I can't sleep on my back—I got up feeling furious. Derek had some damn nerve making up a story about Aidan hurting me and making himself look like some poor victim! Now we were going to have to go to court and fight him *again*. Well, if that's what he wanted, I'd fight him. I'd fight him for Aidan and me.

When I got downstairs, Edie handed me an overnight package from Hawaii. Inside was a small, slightly squashed teddy bear and a note from Colleen.

Dear Piper,
I have covered this bear with kisses and hugged the stuffing out of him because that is what I so long to do to you. It's painful for me to be so far away from you when you need me most, so I hope this bear will transfer some of my emotions from Hawaii to Massachusetts.

I love you so much, Piper, and Rags does too, even if he's not always good at getting the message across. Whatever happens in the future, you can count on us to stand by you always. And the same goes for your

In a Dark Time
(with apologies to Theodore Roethke)

In a dark time I begin to see.
I meet my father in the shady
Undergrowth of lies and charades—
Yes, I have his pedigree.
I live between my memories and his,
That's where I am, that's how it is.

Until I meet a man without a soul
Disguising madness as desire,
Never have I known a liar
so easily pigeonholed.
He teaches me the purity of pure despair.
He's happiest when I panic, scare.

In broad daylight midnight comes again.
I tell myself that I can tell the difference
now between an appetite and romance.
Men like my father, like Aidan,
hide first from guilt and only secondly from me,
but morning comes, and I begin to see.

—*Piper Ragsdale*

friend Aidan. Please tell him we'll do whatever we can to help him. Hawaii is beautiful, but it doesn't hold a candle to my girls!
Love,
Mom

I folded the note and put it in my pocket, then gave the bear a smothering hug. So now I had Colleen's energy to add to my own. Take that, Derek Murphy!

Edie made me eat French toast before she'd let me out the door. "Aren't you afraid I'll get fat?" I asked her.

"I want you to be strong. You're going to have a lot to handle the next few weeks. Even months."

"The trial, you mean?"

"The trial, and also when you go back to school. I doubt that Sam person is the only little idiot in town."

"I'm strong," I told her. "It's easier to be strong when you have a lot of people in back of you. It's Aidan I'm worried about."

She patted the top of my head as she walked in back of me, an unusual gesture of sympathy. "I know, but he has you. And besides, that story Derek made up is obviously a load of bull. No jury will buy it."

"I hope you're right, Grandma."

She lifted her eyebrows at me. "When have I ever not been right?" Then she went to the cupboard, took down a box of Sweet Tooth rejects, and popped one into her mouth—at nine o'clock in the morning!

"He's waiting for you," Adrienne said when I got to her house. "You're right about him, Piper. He's the real deal—I'm crazy about him already."

"Thanks for letting him stay here," I said. "Rags couldn't believe it."

She shook her head. "Your father thinks he's the only one who's allowed to be impulsive. By the way, I called Nathan last night, and he made some phone calls to people he knows. Aidan is all set up with a therapist."

"That was fast."

"Well, we thought this was pretty urgent, what with the trial and everything. His first appointment is Thursday at one o'clock."

"What does Aidan say about it?"

"Oh, he says he's not going, of course. I'm hoping you have more influence over him than I do. You can tell him *you're* going to see somebody."

"I don't have an appointment yet."

"Well, make one. I told Nathan I'd make sure you did."

"Lord, how many parents do I have?"

"As many as you need. Oh, and by the way, I had a talk with Aidan this morning—I'm parenting him a little bit too."

"What do you mean?"

"He's going to stay here in my guest room for a while. When he's back at work, he can pay me a little rent."

"Adrienne! Really?"

"Yes, really. I can use the company, at least until I can talk Gil into moving east. Besides, Aidan is a good kid. Believe me, a kindergarten teacher knows."

I had to hug her. "God, Adrienne, thank you!"

She shooed me away. "Now go upstairs and tell Aidan I'm driving him to therapy on Thursday, and I'm a very cautious driver."

"I don't think riding in a car is his main concern at this point."

"I know, but he has to get over the little hurdles before he can jump the big ones."

Aidan was sitting in a chair in the guest room, dressed in pajamas and a large white terry-cloth bathrobe that must have belonged to Adrienne. He was staring at a book, frowning.

"Hey, you're out of bed!" I said.

"I'm pretending to read." He put the book down.

"I guess that means your headache is better and your eyes are focusing."

"Yeah. It's hard to concentrate though."

"Because of the concussion?"

He shook his head. "Just, you know, everything. Did you hear the stupid story Derek cooked up?"

"Yeah. God, he's such a liar."

Aidan sat forward in the chair, and the book fell to the floor. "He says I hit him, that I hit *you!* There's going to be a *trial.*"

He looked so upset it scared me. What if he tried to run away again? What if I lost him now?

"My grandmother says no jury would ever believe that story. It's obvious he made it up. Besides, there's no knife! And I'll say he's the one who hit me, not you. The trial will be a joke."

He sighed. "No trial is a joke." He wobbled a little as he stood up, and I reached out to help him. "I'm *okay!* I'm just getting back in bed!"

I drew my hands back—Aidan was definitely *not* okay.

"Maybe," I said, thinking as I spoke, "maybe if I dropped

the charges against Derek, he'd drop his charges against you. He probably would. Then we wouldn't have to go to trial."

Aidan glared. "You are not dropping the charges on my account, Piper."

"But then—"

"Then Derek could go out and rape someone else. How would that be? Maybe Rachel or Daisy this time!"

"You're right," I said, lowering my head.

"Of course I'm right," he said, punching his pillows around.

"Are you mad at me?"

"No, I'm just tired of sitting up!" Then he softened a little. "I'm not mad at you, Piper. Why would I be mad at you?"

"Well, for one thing, because you wouldn't be in this mess if it wasn't for me."

He leaned back against the thick pillows Adrienne had propped up for him. "Don't be ridiculous. It's all my fault."

I couldn't believe what I was hearing. "*Your* fault? What part of this is *your* fault? Is it your fault I followed you down the highway? Is it your fault I made Derek furious? Is it your fault he tried to rape me?"

He looked away.

"You think *everything* is your fault! Lord!" I sat down on the end of the bed and felt anger creeping out of some hiding place I hadn't known existed. "You know, I'm getting sick of everybody assigning blame, or trying to grab it for themselves. My mother says it's hers, but Rags wants some too. My sister's ex-boyfriend thinks it's all my fault—and probably a lot of other people do too—but you say it's all yours. Hello! News flash! *It's Derek's fault!* He's the one who's crazy here! He crossed way over the line! *Derek!* Not my parents! Not me! Not you! We may not be perfect, but this is *not our fault!*"

He looked at me seriously. "We all have an effect on each other. We hurt people without meaning to."

I slapped the bedspread. "Absolutely! I agree with you! We do, *without meaning to!* And that's the big difference. Derek *meant* to."

Aidan was quiet for a moment. "Even if you don't *mean* to, you can still do a lot of damage."

"And then, forever after, everything is your fault? Aidan, it just isn't true."

He frowned into his lap. "I suppose now you're going to say I should go talk to that stupid therapist, aren't you? Well, you can give it up, because I'm not going. I can't go, so forget it."

"Well, you need to, whether you want to or not. I have to go to one too. It can't hurt you."

Laughter bubbled in his throat, but it wasn't happy laughter. It had that mean edge, as if he was laughing *at* somebody. Probably himself.

"*Can't hurt me*, did you say? *Can't hurt me?* That's a good one, Piper. *Everything* hurts me! Don't you know that by now? The idea of sitting there and telling some stranger about—" His face turned white and he swallowed hard.

"About what?"

"You know about what."

"You have to talk about it sometime!" I said.

"No, I don't."

"If you don't want to tell a stranger, tell me."

"I'm *not* . . . talking about this, Piper . . . you should go."

223

"I'm not going anywhere. I want to know how it happened. I want you to tell me. Did he run in back of the car as you were pulling out? Was he riding his bicycle? His Big Wheel? How did it happen?"

Aidan stared at me, his eyes enormous, as though he were watching the scene play out in front of him. His mouth quivered, and a shudder ran across his face. Suddenly the words exploded from him.

"No, dammit! He was just sitting there on the driveway drawing with chalk. Brian wasn't doing *anything* wrong, he wasn't running or riding a bike or anything—he was just *sitting* there! And I was in a big hurry—I was always in such a damn big hurry—I was such a *big man*—I had a car now—I had to go pick up my friends—and I jumped in the front seat, slipped it in reverse, and barreled down that driveway without even *looking*, right *over him. I ran over Brian. I fucking smashed the kid!*" He was flooded with tears, choking on them, but still screaming at me. *"So don't fucking tell me it's not my fucking fault!"*

I moved closer so I was sitting next to him, and after a few minutes he leaned against me and let me hold him while he cried. I've seen plenty of people cry before—Daisy, Melissa, Rachel, even my mother—but this was different. It wasn't crying out of sadness—it was from a place most people probably never go; his tears were full of fear and rage and horror, all kneaded into him like yeast into bread. I wondered if he'd ever be able to cry it all out.

I was afraid to say what I had to say, afraid he'd get mad again, but finally I whispered, "It was an accident, Aidan. You didn't mean to do it."

After another minute or two the crying tapered off, and Aidan sat up and pulled away from me. He wiped the edge of the sheet over his glistening face. "Piper," he said, "don't try to fix me. You can't."

I can try, I thought to myself.

"There are other people who want to help you too—not just me. My mother and Nathan. Adrienne—she said you're going to stay here awhile."

He shrugged. "I don't have much choice, do I? I intend to pay her rent as soon as I get back to work."

"Aidan, you have an appointment with a therapist on Thursday. Adrienne wants to drive you. I think you have to go."

He closed his eyes and was quiet for such a long time I was starting to think he'd fallen asleep.

"Aidan?" I whispered.

"I know," he said, without opening his eyes. "I know."

"Will you go? Can I tell Adrienne you'll go?"

He opened his eyes then and stared into mine. "Only if you'll go with me," he said quietly.

When I smiled, his lips cracked open into a lopsided grin. "Nothing I'd rather do," I said.

The Walker

The first time I asked if I could walk
with you, I thought you were a stray
who'd be my aimless pal. Now that
I'm in deep, I see nothing in your life
is peaceful: the whorl of a shell, tire
marks on pavement from a fast car,
a path overgrown with weeds:
they describe you
the way a bomb describes war.

Walking seems to be what's
kept you sane. Like a ghost
you give no explanation
for your wanderings. You're seen
at all hours of the day and night
stalking main streets and back
alleys, climbing to the hillside
cemetery. Lost, walking
keeps you alive, almost.

The turn your life has taken
keeps you up nights. You've caused
so much pain, everything hurts you:
the wrong word, a touch meant to heal,
burns. Yet, this is not the complete
tale. You've taken one life, yes,
but you've saved another. Don't you see?
You've turned again. Now we're both
running in the right direction.

—Piper Ragsdale